Elle Klass

EYE OF THE STORM

EILIDA'S TRAGEDY

VOLUME 1 RUTHLESS STORM TRILOGY

Acknowledgements

Many thanks to all the wonderful people who helped make Eye of the Storm Eilida's Tragedy and the Ruthless Storm Trilogy possible. A special thank you to Marcha Fox for Eilida's Reading and her wonderful astrology knowledge.

Volume 1 Ruthless Storm Trilogy

Books by Elle, Inc.
Published by Books by Elle, Inc.
225 College Dr. #65504
Orange Park, FL 32065
www.elleklass.weebly.com

Author's Disclaimer
This book is entirely fictional. Any characters, places or events are purely figments of the author's imagination. No part of this publication may be reproduced, transmitted or redistributed either in its entirety or in part without the author's express written consent.

Other books by Elle Klass

As Snow Falls

Baby Girl Series:
Book 1-In the Beginning
Book 2 - Moonlighting in Paris
Book 3 - City by the Bay
Book 4 - Bite the Big Apple
Book 5 – Caribbean Heat
Book 6 – Return to the bay
Book 7 – Prison of the Past
Baby Girl Boxes Set Books I-IV

Ruthless Storm Trilogy
Eye of the Storm Eilida's Tragedy Volume 1
Calm before the Storm Evan's Sins Volume 2
In the Midst of the Storm Tommy's Deception Volume 3

Evan's Girls
Scarlett
Emily

The Bloodseekers: St. Augustine Novellas
Book 1 - The Vampires Next Door
Book 2 – The Monster Upstairs
Book 3 – The Ghost Within

hidden journals
Isandro Volume 1

Zombie Girl
Book 1 – Premonition
Book 2 – Infection
Book 3 - Retribution

Volume 1 Ruthless Storm Trilogy

Volume 1 Ruthless Storm Trilogy

Praises

"Pay close attention as Elle Klass tries to strip away your skills to ferret out the answers ahead of time, by creating a whirlwind of action, twisted plotting and pure terror! I love it, I want more, but I admit, I will be sleeping with the lights on for a while as the unknown plays hide and seek with my mind."
Diane at Tome Tender Book Blog

"This psychological paranormal thriller, reminiscent of the "Twilight Zone," is a chilling tale with mystery and intrigue saturating every page."
Author Marcha Fox author of the Star Trails Tetralogy

"It's a Hitchcockian plunge by Ms. Klass, who is once again exploring the world of amnesiac episodes, violent deaths and childhood trauma."
John Reinhard Dizon author of The Triad, Transplant, and Nightcrawler

"Author Elle Klass creates a compelling story using tragedy, survival, guilt, repressed memories, visual triggers and storms to create a tale that encompasses so much more than you expect."
Reader's Favorite

Volume 1 Ruthless Storm Trilogy

"In the first book in The Ruthless Storm Trilogy, Klass's sinister tale is replete with a small but well-developed cast, many of whom function as foils to enhance the principal characters, Eilida and Sunshine. Of course, included in the mix are a tight handful of antagonists who throw all sorts of twists and turns into the plot.."
Anita Lock San Francisco Book Review

"'Twas the Night Before Death"

'Twas the night before death, when all
through the trees,
Not a creature was stirring, not even a flea.
The fireflies buzzed around houses with flare,
In hopes that the Grim Reaper soon wouldn't
be there.
Little Delilah all nestled and snug in her bed,
While visions of a bloody knife circled her
head.
Mamma in her red scarf and dad in his,
Had just been sliced by a razor sharp knife.
When outside the house arose such a clamor,
Delilah sprang from her bed to hide from the
slasher.
Scarlet flowed from around the familiar bed,
Giving way to a flood of crimson and red.
When what to her fearful eyes should appear,
But evil incarnate with a blood tipped dagger.
Shifting and searching not willing to leave,
Little Delilah stayed hidden it must be the
beast.

Prologue

Narrator

Above Eilida's head, the clouds streaked the sky in deep indigo and fuchsias as the sun began to set. In the distance they rumbled in disagreement, slinging squallish threats across the heavens. A mishmash of thoughts coursed through her brain. She thought of work and her boss, how he behaved as a dictator, in a way which was similar to Hitler or Napoleon. He was a small framed man and such as with other men his size, he threw his weight around, leaving her to ponder why all undersized men she knew conducted themselves in that fashion.

Most evenings, Eilida went for walks down the gravel road leading to and from her house. She paused for a moment to smell the honeysuckle growing wild along the roadside. Her mind bantered a concert of short dictators whose worlds unraveled a millennia ago. The wind rushed through the treetops whipping hair across her eyes, momentarily blindfolding her. She smoothed the strands of hair away from her face and looked to the sky. Eilida's train of thoughts shifted from short dictators, replaced by the pending storm cell of doom racing towards her. She contemplated whether or not she had enough time to shower and meet her best friend and roommate, Sage, for their usual Friday night treat, Gino's for live music, beer, and sloppy pizza. Quickening her pace, she hurried home.

Eilida marched around the corner following the gravel road leading to her house. She was about five feet three inches with dark brown hair and a small frame. Her eyes were such a deep and dark blue they appeared black. Sage was a few inches taller with succulent long legs, strawberry blond hair which framed her delicate features, and built like a runway model.

At that very moment, a noise caught her attention. On instinct, she followed the disturbance with her eyes tilting her head towards the direction from which it came. She paused and listened for an instant before continuing her walk, half expecting a fox to be peering coyly through the shrubs or a squirrel or rabbit bounding through the brush. Living high up in the woods, she had grown used to creepy noises which most times were forest creatures. Her home loomed within feet of her; the door knob only a hand's width away.

Once more, she turned her head and focused her attention on the house across the street. For a fraction of a moment, she lingered before continuing inside. She closed and locked the door behind her sure that she was safe from unwanted peril. Gingerly sweeping the curtains aside, she peered through them where she observed the outline of someone walking through her neighbor's living room. She assumed it was nothing more than Mr. Turnwell and dismissed the shadowy figure. Upstairs, she took a shower allowing the warm water to wash off the rest of the stress from her day.

A collection of thoughts about her neighbor's home blasted through her brain. She couldn't place what was off, however, she knew something was different. A steady stream of consciousness cruised through her brain, looking for that one element which wasn't in its place. The cars were parked out front in their usual spots. The plants and lawn were manicured to perfection which she had always thought strange. High up in the mountains most people left their yards to the elements with the exception of keeping their grass mowed and planting bulbs in the spring but not the Turnwell's. Their yard looked like something from a home and garden magazine. Woods surrounded their abode on three sides, the fourth side a gravel road. Who would ever notice their house, except for Eilida, Sage, and the ultra-weird neighbors at the road's end?

Her meditation briefly switched focus to the ultra weirdos. She found them strange, and seriously lacking social skills. They never chirped a hello, or a half-cocked smile, and not once engaged in neighbor-like conversation. They spent an extensive amount of time yelling at each other, *damn stupid bitch-whore*, and her famous comeback *shit for balls asshole*. On occasion they threatened one another or other random creatures, and possessions in their back yard. Other days or nights their patch of Earth sounded like a war zone. The amount of bullets flying from their weapons were highly illegal; nevertheless this never stopped them and with their weirdness, Eilida was not about to say a word because she valued her life and feared they may shoot her and bury her remains deep in the woods where she would never be found. Or worse, leave her to the wolves!

Eilida stepped out of the shower and towel-patted her body, wrapping up her long, dark, wild mane which gave her the appearance of a naked swami. Using a hand towel, she wiped condensation off the mirror and leaned in to apply moisturizer to her face, richly lathering her body in lotion. As she lowered her head to swath her legs in creaminess a shadow passed behind her, although she never noticed as her mind was still focused on the Turnwell's and their perfect yard. She couldn't place her finger on it, but something was amiss, as it yanked and twisted at her guts. She thought the Turnwell's were the epitome of a happy family. They had three small children, two boys ages ten and seven, and a girl not old enough yet for school. They were cordial people, always ready to lend a helping hand. Out in the woods, she knew it was good to have neighbors like them, although she always thought they seemed more like suburban people. They claimed city life was too stressful; too many negative influences were around tempting their young down the wrong paths.

'We want to raise our children in a small town, where everybody knows everybody,' were Mrs. Turnwell's words. 'The woods are peaceful, like heaven in our own backyard,' was Mr. Turnwell's reasoning. Eilida had no children, but understood their sentiment as the children within the community couldn't get into much trouble because everybody knew everybody and many were related in some way.

Eilida finished polishing her hair and face, got dressed and grabbed for her purse. She habitually left her handbag in an exact location and when her hand came up empty, she panicked for a second, until her eyes zeroed in on the familiar fabric bag forming a lump on the sofa. Without giving thought to her purse's strange location, she tossed it over her shoulder as she headed out the door. Her mind was far more occupied with whether or not she would be able to get into town before the storm, as the darkening night sky was moving in at warp speed.

The night sky appeared starless, and thunder continued a forceful battle cry. Her deep sapphire eyes scanned the churning menace above her as she opened her car door. Mid movement her body froze like a deer scanning the forest for predators. Her eyes cemented on the Turnwells' residence. Inside her head the puzzle pieces began to fit, one matching up to the next, until her quandary over the house across the street finally came together. After a few split seconds, she quietly closed her car door with the keys still in her hand, and crept across the street. All the lights were off in the house but one, glowing dimly in the back.

Silently, she stole across the street, but instead of going to the front door, she put her ear up to the wall and listened. From somewhere buried inside her a primordial instinct welled up, which frightened her more than the storm brewing overhead. With her body close to the Turnwells' house and her chest facing out, she advanced to the back. Trembling sobs alternated with short, shallow breaths told her ears that a small child was wailing inside. Her eyes caught sight of a dim light shining from the door which had been left open a crack. As she slid along the wall of the house. The back deck steps unfolded in front of her. She cocked her head, glancing towards the window and slowly progressed up the steps without a creak, something like a cat stalking its prey. As she reached the final step, she melted along the wall until her head became flush against the door frame. Taking a deep and silent breath; her guts inside wrenching and twisting, she peered inside through the cracked door, gasping at the scene before her eyes. Eilida tore down the steps at warp speed, descending the tree stuffed mountain, while tears cascaded violently down her cheeks.

Thoughts raged through her brain, churning and contorting. Her legs charged down the mountain as if on auto-pilot. The horrific scene inside the house played like a broken record in her head. Tree branches tore at her clothes and scratched at her flesh as she dashed down the ridge. She barely felt them stinging as her mind was too consumed by the vivid spectacle she had witnessed inside the Turnwells' home. Bleeding gashes covered her arms, face, and legs. Gnarled tree branches grew arms, jutting into the path before her eyes. The rain began to pour across her forehead, leaving flowing rivulets washing away her tears and blood. Chunks of hair plastered against her face.

The solid earth had become bombarded with water rushing hard under her feet, causing her to slip in its wetness. Eilida reached her hand out for something to grab hold of but the trees curled in their disfigured appendages while her feet slipped further beneath; digging into the wet savage ground. Desperate mud covered hands penetrated the sludge groping for a large tree root. Her feet sank further into the ooze until they hit a large rock, sending Eilida flying, like an unwanted toy, down the ridge. Tree trunks and small rocks got their licks in bouncing her to and fro. The inertia of her body halted by a large boulder nestled beside the river, leaving her petite frame motionless against the flooding rains. A mess of blood curled and flowed from her head, leaving tributaries along her cheek. Shreds of fabric that used to be clothing clung to her bloody skin as the shadowy moonlight bathed her immobile and unconscious body.

Sunshine

Warm rays soaked Sunshine's body, as she stretched her entire length, welcoming the alluring morning light. The children would soon be walked to the bus stop, their watchful mothers in tow, drinking morning coffee and discussing neighborhood gossip - new happenings at school, church, their afternoon schedules, taking their children to dance, and ball games. She always loved mornings, and couldn't remember a day when the sun didn't shine. Life had always been good to her. In her mind, she had the perfect job working as a receptionist at a local newspaper, The Lyden Times.

Joe (her boss) says, "Your name fits you, as you bring sunshine into every day."

On a normal morning, she arrived to work eight forty five on the dot, even though her regular hours started at nine. Quickly, she would place her purse in her desk drawer and begin her morning ritual of getting coffee ready for everyone. This activity gave her a sense of importance and purpose in a hectic office, most people scrambled in half awake, needing a morning perk, and so she loved it.

Her co-workers generally rolled in around nine o'clock, looking forward to her coffee, complimenting, "I couldn't make it through the morning without my cup of Joe." She believed in quality over quantity, insisting on a pricey brew.

When finished, she'd return to her desk and greet everyone with a smile; like a belle in a festive parade. Next, she'd wait for the phone to ring, and her employers to start making requests of her. There was always work to be completed, therefore she never sat idly at her desk, fussing with her nails, or makeup as she had seen so many other receptionists do. Today was a Monday, meaning the reporters would kick off with a meeting which on most occasions lasted about an hour, which was her slow time. Afterwards a constant flow of work and before she knew it, five o'clock would arrive, informing her that it was time to pack up and go home.

Today, though, had not been a typical day, so let's rewind. When Sunshine walked into the office at eight forty-five, the office swarmed with activity; breaking news didn't manage on a nine-to-five schedule, as Sunshine did. The past weekend had been one of those times. Sunshine's foolproof life was fashionably distorted from reality, making her feel out of sorts with the extensive buzz and commotion surrounding her. A constant flow of discussion, vigorous fingers tapping across keyboards, rivaled only by the swoosh and the beeping of printers filling the air, while her colleagues bustled around.

She composed herself, running her palms down her impeccably ironed pin skirt and flipping her hair back. She maneuvered to the coffee pot. The current pot emptied, except for a brown sludge jiggling at the bottom. The table it sat on covered in sugar, dribbles of creamer, and used coffee stirs lined the trash can. She busied herself with a new pot, and cleaning the mess left behind from her co-workers. Unsure how her associates managed without her, she imagined most of them lived in messy homes.

"Sunshine, you're a dream, what would we do without you?"

Déjà vu, she thought as the words spilled from Joe's mouth.

She navigated through the chaos taking place at her desk. Seconds later, Samantha approached her; Sunshine's other boss, next in line to Joe, "I need you to get on the phone with the florist and have a bouquet of flowers sent to the hospital. A young woman was found in the forest, not too far outside the city. She is approximately twenty two, twenty three years old, she lost her footing in a bad rain storm, plummeting to the foot of Mount Wilde, crashing into a boulder resting beside River Freedom. She's been brought here, to our hospital, and is in intensive care, room one twenty three." The words ran out of her mouth faster than the speed of sound, and her temple pulsed at a rapid rhythm under her skin.

Samantha was an intense career oriented individual who always dressed to the nines, trails of expensive perfume saturated the air wherever she went, and she wore her henna hair wrapped in a contemporary bun. After Samantha had finished barking orders at her, she left, and Sunshine got on the phone and took care of the flowers.

At noon, Jerry, Sunshine's boyfriend of two plus years, stopped in at newspaper headquarters to take Sunshine to lunch, as was their ritual. Average in height with light ginger hair, mixed with sun kissed blond, not a strand out of place, and dimples riding each side of his mouth; Jerry was an attractive man. They went to lunch daily, he brought her fresh cut flowers once a week, which she placed meticulously around her desk. The fragrance delighted her senses.

Jerry is Sunshine's Mr. Perfect, an anomalous complement to her. At lunch, they talk about their mornings, evening plans - usual lovebird chit chat. This Monday morning Sunshine barely had time to breathe, let alone eat; by twelve twenty, her stomach was growling with anticipation of food. She flung her purse over her shoulder, and they left for lunch.

"I've never seen your office such a hubbub of activity," Jerry commented.

"A young woman was found over the weekend, her injuries so bad they rushed her to the hospital here. Lyden has had an outpouring of concern for her. I've been glued to the telephone. I am starving," drawing out the words I am to emphasize she wanted to eat first, talk later.

Upon leaving the restaurant, Sunshine spotted a young woman at a corner table by herself. Her posture slumped, head bent towards the ground with long, dense black waves of hair masking any features that may have been identified underneath. The sight of the woman elicited feelings of sorrow and loneliness inside Sunshine. The harried events of the day had left her with an overwhelming compassion for this young lady, who she assumed had been stood up by a nameless man.

As the couple exited the restaurant, clouds moved in blackening the sky. Once inside the car, the heavens gave way to an afternoon shower; a fitting end to lunch on such a hectic day, even so, there's never a drop of rain in Sunshine's world. As soon as she acknowledged the shower, it was gone and within a few minutes everything dried up, the brilliant sphere in the sky was back out in force.

Her private thoughts registering the strangeness of the weather; she was unable to recall even a slight drizzle in her presence. The last rain the city endured had been months ago when Jerry took her to the Bahamas. The Lyden Times weatherman had informed her that stratus clouds covered the sky in a dark, week-long vigil of perpetual steady showers.

Back at work Sunshine went about her day, smiling as usual. She had been able to pick up on a few more details about the young woman, such as her dark hair color, and unknown identity. Sunshine's heart went out to her, but she was consumed with work, and settled for completing her job as the best course of action to help the injured woman.

Jerry came by her apartment that evening and the couple prepared chicken casserole, and salad. While cutting the vegetables, her voice laced with concern she mentioned, "They haven't identified the young woman yet, so many people keep calling, churches are taking monetary donations, the paper is assisting in trying to find her name, and family. It's really beautiful how everyone is reaching out to her."

Jerry placed the casserole in the oven and took her hand, accompanying her to the couch. "Exactly what I love about you; always putting others first. Your day has been swamped, and tomorrow you can do more to help but you need a fresh mind." He put a movie in the DVD player, and gingerly grabbed her ankles, lifting them in his lap. After their dinner and the movie, he gave her a goodnight kiss before heading home.

Tuesday came, the hype at Sunshine's work had continued with a vengeance. The entire city was pulling money and resources for the young lady and Sunshine found herself inundated with phone calls. Multi-tasking wasn't an option but a necessity - as she answered one line, another would start ringing, when she had them on hold, a different line would blink, and another.

While answering half a dozen calls consecutively, she managed to text Jerry not to meet her for lunch; she had decided to work through it. Assisting people whenever able was a moral obligation to Sunshine, keeping karma on an even keel. She couldn't think of any worthier cause than helping a young lady not unlike herself, who'd had such an unfortunate calamity.

Jerry stopped by her office for lunch bringing her a sub from her favorite shop, Hoagie World. All their breads were made fresh daily and they had a myriad of assorted toppings to choose from. Her most cherished was Chicken Caesar on flat bread, loaded with onions, romaine lettuce, black olives, tomatoes, topped with provolone, and a dash of Caesar. She didn't want the extra calories from the dressing, but loved the taste. Jerry knew her well, and affectionately thought of her when purchasing. The phone planted on one ear, she mouthed a thank you, placing the bag on top of her desk, she blew him a kiss which he caught and returned.

She reached her hand inside the bag, extracting the chicken Caesar along with a note; it read *Love you, see you tonight*. Her lips parted into a smile watching Jerry walk down the steps of the building. She placed the note inside her purse, allowing the phones to ring, as her mind floated into a romantic daydream.

The sun fell low on the horizon, iridescent layers covered the atmosphere, alerting Sunshine evening was approaching. Her eyes glanced at the round, mechanical clock, hanging lopsided on the wall, as the minute hand clicked into the five o'clock position. Sunshine trudged her weary body to her compact car, heels clicking as she went. While she fumbled around in her purse for car keys, a lipstick fell from the opening. Still a few feet from her car, she leaned down to retrieve her frosted ice lipstick and caught sight of a pair of muddy running shoes. Mucky frazzled jeans covered the tops and were standing on the opposite side of her car.

An unnatural, eerie silence fell upon the garage creating a vacuum; the only sound that she could hear was the thumping of her heart beat. A creepy feeling swept over her while fear mixed with familiarity wrenched at her internal organs, causing shallow breaths to escape her mouth, and a quickening of her pulse. She cautiously lifted her eyes upwards to see the mysterious stranger; to her surprise, not a soul was standing there, and the muddy shoes had disappeared. She twirled herself around, but nobody was in sight.

She plucked her lipstick off the garage floor and beeped her car. Her heart beat wildly in her chest, knocking to get free of her body, *thump, thump, thump.* Wasting no time, she ran the few feet left to her car, jumped inside, and locked the doors. Her deep blue eyes scanned the garage, looking for the perpetrator. She gathered herself together, taking a deep breath, knowing she still had to check the seat behind her. She took a deep breath, closed her eyes, and gradually turned her head to peer at the seat behind her. She fully expected to see a maniacal killer raising his arms with a plastic bag in his hands to suffocate her. Finding the back seat empty, Sunshine placed her palm over her heart, and a flood of air emerged from her lips as she released her breath.

She cranked the engine, and the tires chirped as her vehicle leapt from its parking spot. An isolated rumble of thunder let loose as she made a right turn out of the garage, a single dark cloud, hung in the sky, following her home.

The ordeal mixed with feelings of fear had left an impression in her mind as she headed towards her apartment. The small muddy shoes tarried on the tip of her thoughts, then like a bombshell she realized they were female shoes. Not wanting to believe what she had seen she dismissed it, assuming she'd been working too hard without accumulating enough sleep.

The remainder of the week continued nearly as hectic for Sunshine. Jerry had brought her lunch daily, although they barely had enough time to squeeze in conversational niceties. The past week at work she had become gopher extraordinaire, running across the street for bagels, sandwiches, ordering pizza, and Chinese. She even stopped at the pharmacy for Joe, picking up his heart pressure medication. All the while she learned nothing more about the young lady.

She took a good look at her workspace before leaving Friday evening. Ordinarily, her desk was a picture of organization, but now looked as though a tornado had ravaged it. Pens, her message pad, and tablets of paper were strewn about, with a layer of crumbs settled beneath. Twisting her lips and wrinkling her straight-edged nose into a snub, she began purging her desk of filth and reconstructing.

Old messages cluttered the floor around her escritoire where the draggletail reporters missed, while aiming for the waste basket. She scrunched down the contents of the trashcan using her foot, and began throwing in the balled up papers. One stuck to her hand, which she waved fervently to remove, after several swings the small paper flew off, onto her desk. Grossed out by the residue left behind, she dumped and rubbed in a load of sanitizer on her hands.

As she slathered the sanitizer, the message on the note caught her eye, it read *Sandy*, but wasn't in her handwriting. In fact, she didn't recognize the writing. The week had been a flurry, and anybody could have written the message; the word Sandy was meaningless. She took two pencils, used them as chopsticks, raised the note between them, and tossed it into the trash.

Eilida

Bits and pieces glistened through my head, yearning to break the surface. My body felt as though I was gliding weightless through a vast space. Fluorescent lights flickered above me and distorted voices hovered close, their faces long and misshapen as if I were looking at them through carnival funhouse mirrors.

"Ill..id..a," every syllable elongated. A bright light flashed into my eyes, leaving behind a trail of colors. A face swam into view, its forehead and chin small, cheeks stretched like a rubber band.

The sounds got louder, and an enormous commotion surrounded me. I wiggled my fingers which sent a searing pain through my arm, unwilling to let that stop me. I needed to leave, forcing my torso upwards, nothing happened. I couldn't move. Panic rushed up my spinal cord aching to get free. A loud, unfriendly beep wailed through my ears, then, blackness crept across my eyes starting from the corners and catching up in the middle.

Laughter and Wine

Narrator

She entered her apartment by six twelve. Discombobulated from the week, she had forgotten to check her mail. Running back downstairs, she opened her mailbox; the cargo inside nothing but junk, which she tossed into the recycle receptacle and marched back upstairs. She hadn't made it up the fourth step when a child's giggle teased her eardrums. She turned her head to the direction of the sound, anticipated seeing a young girl playing with a toy doll or stuffed animal, and having to walk them back to their parents. She was stunned when no child was present; so, she bent down and searched within the small confines of the entry until she was satisfied she was alone. Knowing her mind was frazzled she finished her trek back upstairs, locked the door behind her, kicked off her shoes, and plummeted to the couch, tossing the mass of blankets lying on the backrest over her body. She fell into a deep sleep.

Her body wrenched and thrashed as she dreamt, "Look hole," her arms lifting uniformly above her head, as if she was holding something up. "Me too, Sanny," she contorted her body and mimicked grabbing a box and pulling it open. "It loud, mommy?" Finally, resting her body in a fetal position she sobbed softly.

Awoken when her body slipped off the couch, crash landing on her cell phone, which buzzed wildly beneath her and the mess of blankets. She fumbled underneath of her until she had the buzzing phone in her hand, looking at the number she immediately dialed back, "Jerry… I was so tired, I must have fallen asleep on the couch… it is." Her eyes peered towards the windows, as she rose and padded towards them. The phone in one hand, she slid open the curtains with the other, "Uh-huh… I'll be ready, love you." She remembered nothing of her dream.

Within twenty minutes Jerry had picked her up and they were on the road watching it unfold before them. She enthusiastically declared to Jerry, "I love the drive and really can't wait to see your parents again." Suburbia disappeared and opened up to the woods and blooming flowers.

Jerry's hands were on the wheel and his lips curled into a smile as he said, "They love you, too. This weekend I have something planned for you." She adored his surprises, and happy butterflies welled up inside her.

An hour later, Jerry's car swung around the horseshoe drive lined with azaleas that curved along his parents' home's sprawling yard. Plantation style large white columns supported a wrap-around porch which cascaded before her eyes. On the porch was a large variation of potted flowers, a porch swing, and a small table with a couple of chairs on either side. His parents greeted them with hugs and kisses.

"Let me help with those," said his father grabbing the bag from Sunshine's hand.

"Thank you," she whispered planting a kiss on his cheek. "This week has been so incredibly busy at work I am so glad to be here." All smiles, the happy family disappeared into the house.

His father, Mr. Butler, was not an exceptionally tall man and he wore a little extra weight around the belly. His hair was the same color as unburned charcoal with a couple white strips offsetting the bald spot he carried on top of his head. His jaw was square and taut, giving him a stern appearance. His mother had a small frame with a similar roundness to that of his father protruding her mid-section. Her eyes were almost perfect circles, deep brown streaks of grey highlighted her chocolate hair, mostly around her face. Altogether they were ordinary to look at; their hearts were made of gold.

The house sported a grand foyer with marble tile, a crystal chandelier hung from the cathedral ceiling, and a spiral staircase surrounded the foyer leading the way to several bedroom suites. To the left of the stairs stood a formal dining room, which was attached to the kitchen, and opened up to the wraparound porch. A large parlor for guests was located to the right and next to that a smaller game room. It was a magnificent house and Sunshine loved it along with loving his parents, and they loved her. She was, most definitely, a ray of sunshine.

Sunshine was curious what Jerry had planned and felt as though she was going to burst open in anticipation. Her mind reminisced over all the sweet surprises Jerry had showered her with, as she sat on the back porch sipping lemonade with Jerry's mom. The back yard was as impressive as the front. Hypericum, northern bayberry, and butterfly bushes neatly outlined the porch; flowering dogwood and Redbud trees accented the borders, mixed with willow trees for shade, and bleeding hearts bloomed beautifully underneath.

At the end of the property was a short wooden dock jutting over their private lake. "We have been working on the path to the lake. Last time you were here, it was full of ruts, but we smoothed them out, planted some new honeysuckle. I'm afraid it will grow like wildfire, but I love the scent."

Hearing the lake mentioned made Sunshine remember the picnic Jerry had taken her on when they first met. It had been a glorious sunny day. The weather was warm, but not too hot. She wore a floral print sleeveless dress. They had sat on a blanket and ate tiny tuna finger sandwiches, watermelon, and finished the meal with pound cake. "You will have to take a walk out there later with Jerry," encouraged Mrs. Butler.

Sunshine's mind flashed back to the present, "We will, of course." As the two women continued to talk, Jerry and his father joined in.

"It's been busy, do tell," piped Mr. Butler senior.

"A young woman has been found badly injured. She had no identity on her." As Sunshine spoke, something clung to the back of her brain just out of reach.

"I've read about situations like that, sad thing." His father replied, shaking his head in empathy.

Jerry took Sunshine's hand and looked to his parents, "We're taking a walk to the lake." His parents smiled and glanced at each other. Sunshine didn't notice their glances as she wrapped her hand around Jerry's.

Sun bathed the path and honeysuckle scented the air. Appearing like a mirror, the lake illuminated before them. With her hand in his, they walked across the dock, dropping their feet into the tepid water.

Jerry motioned to the edge of the dock where wild flowers grew, "What's that?"

"Not sure," she answered, cocking her head towards the object and squinting her eyes against the sun's radiance reflecting off of it. "It's shiny and look, a rainbow forms around it!"

Jerry looked towards the glowing item, knowing full well what the object was, he continued his ploy, "I don't see the rainbow."

"You're not looking right. Tilt your head like this." Placing her hands around his face, she carefully angled it. "Can you see it now?"

"No," angling his head a little more, "Yup, I see it!"

"It looks like diamonds in the grass," she announced. Curious what was causing the illusion she stood up and advanced towards it. "Oh, oh," she stammered drawing her hands over her mouth in astonishment, leaning down she picked up the tiny shiny object. Between her thumb and forefinger, she held a gold band adorned with a colossal diamond. "Yes, oh my gosh, yes!" Tears of joy filled her eyes as she scampered to his side. "I love you," she said as she wrapped her tiny arms around his back and placed a giant kiss on his lips.

"Sunshine, you are my sunshine. You make the sun come out during the day and the stars shine bright at night. I want to wake and go to bed every day for the rest of my life with you. Will you marry me?" He asked while getting on one knee, and slipping the ring onto her awaiting finger.

The anticipation now over, she knew his surprise and her heart skipped several beats as she contemplated being Mrs. Jerry Butler. "Yes, yes, yes, you are my rock and my joy." The newly engaged couple merged their arms and lips around one another in a long lasting kiss.

Over dinner, they told Jerry's parents who couldn't have been happier, although they knew all along. Jerry had informed his parents of his plan and his mother had actually planted the ring earlier in the day knowing just the spot that would catch the most sunlight. His parents thought of her as the daughter they never had and could find no imperfections within her.

His parents had planned a feast for the evening consisting of Chicken Marsala adorned with mushrooms, rice pilaf, and fresh asparagus with a Pinot Noir to top off the meal. Taper candles poised in brass holders embellished the cream lace table cloth, covering the antique thick oak table. Laughter, wedding stories and preparations filled the air. June thirtieth had been chosen for the wedding date and his parents had suggested having the ceremony and reception at their house. Sunshine loved their house and always felt most safe and comfortable within its walls. She couldn't think of anywhere else on the planet that she would rather be married and graciously accepted their offer.

The celebration moved outside beneath the stars that seemed to twinkle brighter that night as if sending their approval. Fireflies glowed just as brightly, twinkling amongst all the greenery - blinking as Earthbound stars. The wine flowed freely and Sunshine melted into the mood, no longer sipping at it, but drinking candidly, as did everyone else. From her spot on the porch, she caught sight of a shadow passing through the trees, however she quickly let go of the thought as her inebriated mind had little focus. Instead of worry she felt joy. The night wrapped up about midnight as the slightly intoxicated family rose from their chairs and shuffled inside. A warm breeze blew across her back followed by a chill making the hairs along her arms stand at attention, met with a wave of goosebumps. She shivered and brought her arms around her chest, rubbing her shoulders for warmth.

Sunshine and Jerry didn't believe in sex before marriage. They believed it was a gift of exceptional value only to be given to that one special person so they occupied separate rooms during the night. In her chambers, she slipped into a soft cotton nightgown and snuggled into bed. Her eyes flickered and then, sleep was upon her. At nearly three in the morning she arose, still asleep, from her bed, clutching the down comforter she drifted towards the closet, slid open the doors and snuggled into a corner; the thick blanket nestled beside her.

The following morning as the sun rose and illuminated her room a tinge of panic rushed across her spine as she opened her eyes, realizing straight away that she wasn't snuggled in bed. Her mind confused, she held the comforter close, glimpsing the small compartment she was curled up in. Finally, it dawned on her that she was in the closet, but couldn't figure out how or why she had gotten there. She crawled out of her corner and carefully lifted the bedding which she returned to its rightful place on the bed. Inside her head was a flutter of activity, as she attempted to piece together what happened. Unable to make neither heads nor tails of it, she relented to blaming the wine which she had overindulged in the previous night.

The rest of the day she chose to think about getting married. Gleefully, she ignored the strange events that had occurred over the past few days. Strange incidents didn't happen in the black and white structure of her life. She and Jerry's mom began a rough draft of wedding plans.

At sunset, Jerry and Sunshine said their goodbyes to his parents and were back on the road in order to make work on Monday. He turned on the radio and soft rock played quietly while Sunshine dozed on and off.

Interference

By Monday, the hype at the Lyden Times had slowed; Sunshine used the opportunity to ask about the mystery woman, partially out of concern and partially her own curiosity. "Have you learned anything new?" She inquired of Joe while handing him a hot cup of fresh coffee.

He barely peeked up at her from the pile of papers and files scattered across his desk, as he mumbled, "We know she had no ID on her and evidently can't remember a thing. The doctors are saying that's normal with a blow to the head like that. They expect she'll get it back in time. The police canvassed the area, but nobody recognized her description."

"Someone must know her. If she can't remember and the police can't identify her then what will happen to her? Where will she go when she is released? She can't stay at the hospital forever. She must be terrified!" Rolling around in Sunshine's head were feelings she might have in the same situation as the young lady.

Sensing the desperation in her voice he provided her with his full attention and responded, "Whoa, whoa slow down, it's awful, but I'm sure her memory will come back and there is no shortage of people trying to help her out."

"I couldn't imagine what it would be like to have no memories, it's just so awful. I may take a little longer for lunch today. I want to stop at the hospital and bring her some flowers," she stated matter of factly.

"Fine by me, take as much time as you need," Joe replied immediately burying his head back into his work. ·

"Thanks," Sunshine's eagerness coupled with her overwhelming compassion took control, and she wanted to right every wrong that had devastated the young woman's life.

Jerry hadn't taken two steps inside the newspaper headquarters when Sunshine ran over to him announcing, "Can we grab a quick bite for lunch today and stop at the florist and then the hospital? I want to bring that young woman some flowers, maybe brighten her day and maybe…" The words ran out of her mouth like a waterfall.

Putting his fingers to her lips, he responded, "Yes, whatever you want."

Hugging him she stated, "You are the absolute best! I keep thinking about how lonely she must be, and how frightened she must feel."

Sunshine

I grabbed the friendliest bouquet of brilliant yellow lilies mixed with white daisies. Most assuredly she would like it and hopefully, it would bring happiness into her day.

The hospital loomed ahead, four stories surrounded by a semi-white exterior with the regimented flowers and trees surrounding it. "Oh… I forgot her room number," I whimpered.

"I'm sure they will know inside, dear."

"But it was there a minute ago, I just forgot it now. This very second."

"You may be a ray of sun and beauty but you're not infallible." He was right, but how could I forget from one second to the next? My mind has always been sharp as a tack.

At the front desk, we were greeted by a thirtyish woman with a round face, plump body accented by teddy bear scrubs, and her hair in a bob. She smiled, "You look lost. Can I help you?" She seemed to zone in on my forgetfulness which made me feel as big as a speck of dust.

"We are here to see the young woman who was found last week."

"Yes, she has had many flowers. Her room was changed recently, give me a minute." She clicked on the keyboard a few times, her eyes scanning the computer screen, "She's in room three twelve."

"Thank you," I said. She smiled again, in fact, she had smiled the whole time, and suddenly it was like I was living in a cartoon and not reality. The walls around me looked imperfect, almost two dimensional.

The elevator glided to a stop and the heavy metal doors opened up on both sides. Three people walked out and we and an orderly with a cart entered. "What floor?" Jerry asked the orderly.

"Four," he responded.

Jerry punched both numbers and the elevator began to climb. I suddenly felt cold and the air around me began spinning as if a tornado had locked itself in the elevator with us. Before my eyes, the walls vanished, they were replaced with darkness and howling air swirling from all directions, becoming so strong I struggled to keep my ground. I finally lost the battle and was blown backward. My eyes blinded by the darkness, my ears deafened by the rumbling, and my body feeling only the rushing, spinning air around it. I felt defenseless.

Exploring the air around me with my hands I reached into the funneling winds which had swallowed me. A desperate need filled me up inside to hold on to something that would keep me from being blasted into the oblivion. I knew Jerry was there somewhere, but I couldn't feel him or anything solid. The sheer strength of the storm lifted my body further and I began twisting with it like a ballerina in an out of control pirouette. Suddenly, the tornado vomited me out and sent me crashing into something hard. The darkness disappeared, overcome by bright hospital lights and the wind had dissipated, leaving my helpless form lying belly up across the hall floor with both feet inside the elevator.

"Sunshine, Sunshine," Jerry was on his knees pleading with me. His eyebrows scrunched into thin lines with worry wrinkles covering his forehead.

"I'm okay. I tripped." I managed to eke out. My mind still hazy from the illusion.

Jerry grasped my hands and carefully pulled me to safety, as if I was a fragile porcelain doll, "That didn't look like a trip, you suddenly just fell backward."

"Really, you're making too much of it." The words flew out of my mouth with harshness. What was wrong with me? What had happened in the elevator? My gluteus maximus ached with pain! I didn't want to answer any more questions as I had no idea how to begin describing the terror I felt, and why it happened. Jerry seemed to understand my tone and complied.

I felt like a complete bumbling klutz, nothing like myself. I had taken ballet for many years and was as graceful as a swan, or had I? My memories eluded me again, twice now today. I knew I had taken ballet, but couldn't remember a single lesson. At this moment, I was glad that Jerry had the bouquet and not me or the flowers would be all over the floor. As we drew nearer her room my legs grew rubber-like and I wrapped my arm around Jerry just in case I had another episode.

She wasn't in the room. Having experienced enough adventure in the hospital for one day, I placed the flowers on a nightstand beside her bed near a well-worn and very well loved brown monkey. Somewhere in my frazzled memories he sprang forward. How could I remember him and not my beloved ballet shoes? I know I must have had a pair but right now this monkey played around my mind jumping from tree to tree.

"You must have just missed her," said a short, bald doctor with tiny black eyes, a Cheshire cat grin, and donning the usual blue scrubs.

"Has she been moved again?" asked Jerry.

My entire body now felt shaky and everything in the room seemed to shift in front of my eyes, like an old TV with bad reception. I blinked, hoping to shift it all back, no luck - everything remained distorted.

One more try, I closed my eyes and took a deep breath while I heard the doctor say, "She's out for another CAT scan I believe, she should be back soon." When I reopened my eyes the room was normal and the doctor was gone.

I felt as though I was in an episode of the twilight zone. What would be next?

"Do you want to wait?"

"No," judging by Jerry's expression I was a little too quick on the draw so I followed up with, "I've been gone too long. I know Joe said take as long as I need but I don't want to take advantage of his kindness either."

"Alright, we can come back another day, maybe in the evening?"

Knowing I never wanted to step foot in the hospital of horrors again, although not wanting to sound ungrateful or anxious, I replied, "We'll play it by ear. Let's not take the elevator. I think I would rather get some exercise and walk." Truly, I just plain didn't want to get into that elevator again; getting blown out the door was enough excitement for one day. I feared the next time it might blow through the roof or take a free fall into the basement.

My legs remained unstable until we got down to the first floor. That was a feat, managing stairs with jelly legs but I got through it. Jerry glanced at me oddly from time to time, but he didn't ask. I assumed his mind was pondering my curious behavior.

Outside the hospital, life seemed to become reality again with the exception of a few black clouds emerging from behind the structure. The eerie scene made the hospital appear like a crazy mental institution from a horror movie. It looked like the kind where the doctors electrocute and torture their patients, and then, the patients turn on them. Everyone ends up dying and their agonized souls roam the halls for eternity. What was I thinking? *I had never even seen a horror flick, had I?*

At the office, I relished the comfort of my plush computer chair. The phone buzzed, and the small screen told me it was Joe. "Hello?"

"I got a cart of files in here for you."

"Be right there." I looked at my desk, which already had a pile that had grown last week when I had barely enough time to answer the swarm of phone calls let alone anything else. Instead of feeling overwhelmed, I decided monotonous work was what Dr. Sunshine called for right now. Happy and feeling like myself, I strolled into his office.

"How was the hospital?" He asked.

It was an innocent question I know, but it was one that I really didn't want to answer. "We dropped off the flowers, but she wasn't in the room. I think the doctor said a CAT scan?" I wrapped my hands around the cart, not wanting to discuss the details, and started pushing towards the door.

"CAT scan huh? The talk is, her body is in bad shape, broken bones, deep gashes," he articulated in an experienced way.

"I didn't get to see her…" my voice trailed off. I had almost slipped and said, because the hospital gave me the creeps. Not a *me* statement at all which made my arm hairs salute. It was like someone else was in my brain. "I better get these filed along with the pile already on my desk. Maybe, you should make a visit?" I suggested.

"My wife went last week. Says she's bandaged everywhere, could barely see her face," he revealed leaning back into his worn pleather chair.

"Really, your wife went, why didn't you say anything?"

Raising his bushy eyebrows, he replied, "Busy," in a nondescript tone.

"Right, which is exactly what I need to be right now," I said, as I exited his office.

"Maybe I will," he uttered as I wheeled the cart out. My caboose was still sore.

At home, I ran a hot bath with plenty of Epsom salts, allowing them to ease away the pain in my tail. The heat from the water absorbed through my skin, which felt like heaven to my aching body. Soon my subconscious began to dwell on the peculiar events in my recent life; the memories of muddy shoes, sleeping in the closet, and the elevator incident danced through my head. What did any of it mean? I had heard of people who went crazy because of brain tumors… In that moment of intense reflection my phone blasted, "Hey There Delilah" by the Plain White T's.

At the sound, I nearly jumped straight out of the tub like a cat that just got sprayed with water. I didn't have a fancy ringtone on my phone. My feet dripping in bubbles and H2O caused me to slip when they hit the tile floor, and I slid into the door. Luckily, I was able to grasp the handle, while my feet scrambled to keep me upright. After several seconds of running in place I regained composure and saved myself the pain of falling backwards and reinjuring my tush.

I patted my hands dry and checked my phone, not one phone call registered on the log. Cold shivers raced up and down my spine, and a spooky mist formed from the evaporating water of my bath curling together, forming the shape of a woman. It then dissolved. Was my mind playing tricks on me? *Did I really see a form… no couldn't be.*

Even worse than my recent clumsy mishaps and ghostly mist was the wind which howled all night nearly blowing Jerry up the stairs to my apartment and yanking the door right out of his hands, slamming with a loud thud.

Instead of cooking, he brought Chinese. Unsure what came over me, I suddenly didn't like eating with chopsticks. Tonight I took three bites with them and went to the kitchen for a fork; bringing back two.

"Tonight we're going to eat this with silverware." I placed a fork in front of him and extracted the chopsticks right out of his hands with a piece of orange chicken between them. I wrapped my teeth around the chicken and set the chopsticks down. Jerry just sat and looked at me with astonishment plastered across his face.

"You… never… told me you… didn't like chopsticks?" he said stumbling on the words.

Without thinking, I responded, "I don't remember." I stabbed a couple shrimp and said, "Tonight we eat with forks." His face grew more puzzled, as did my mind. We ate in quiet; the dumbfounded expression never left his face.

The Grey

The following day, I parked in the garage as usual, which continued to send chills down my spine after the muddy shoe incident. I made sure I parked close to the door so I wouldn't have far to walk in the evening. Shifting the gear into park my phone started buzzing with a message from Joe *pick up bagels across the street*. The order had already been placed and paid. I was just doing the gopher work which as of lately had been a larger part of my job than usual. The order consisted of four full bags with various cream cheeses.

Carefully, I balanced everything; the bagel bags gripped in my left hand, and my purse over my shoulder, feeling something like *The Cat in the Hat*. I pressed the walk button with my right hand. The light changed, and I cautiously proceeded into the crosswalk. From the back someone smashed into me sending me and the bagels flying, luckily the bags were sealed tight. A young woman in a black hoodie hurried past me without so much as an apology. The hood draped across her head hid any facial features, although wisps of raven black hair flowed from under the hood, the wind catching them in her haste.

My butt was still sore from the hospital, however I willed myself off the ground feeling something like an old woman with arthritis. "Let me help you?" asked a friendly voice belonging to a fiftyish woman in a business suit. She picked up a couple bags and finished walking across the street with me. On the opposite side of the street, she handed them back and asked, "Are you alright?"

"Yes, and thank you. I can't believe how rude that woman was! Lucky, they sealed them tight or there would be bagels everywhere." I replied with a gentle forced laugh.

"Oh," she said, her eyes scanning the area. "Are you sure? You got to watch that pothole on the other side, gets people every time." She smiled and walked off.

Pothole? I questioned to myself, surveying the area where I had fallen. Sure enough, a small one existed, large enough to catch the heel of a shoe. It hadn't been what forced my trip. I had felt the pressure on my back when she carelessly ran into me, and now I felt a tinge of mystery, wondering how she had vanished so quickly without "Business Suit Lady" noticing her.

I decided not to linger on it anymore and allow a curt bitch to ruin my day. Wow! That was not my thought; voices were in my head, thinking for me. Above, ominous clouds moved in, darkening the sun, threatening rain. That would be a fitting beginning to this already ghastly day. Again, not my thought, the voice inside was thinking for me. My watch said eight fifty which meant I had wasted enough time. Hauling myself as expediently as I was able to handle with four bagel bags and an extremely sore bum, I maneuvered the steps leading into the Lyden Times.

The clouds clung to the sky all morning and a vapor seemed to rise from the ground. Normally, they blew off in other directions, but not today. They lingered for most of the morning but dropped no rain. It was nearly lunch by the time they burned off and the sun was back; bold and brilliant in the day sky.

Samantha, dressed in a dark blue dress suit and three inch heels, clacked her way over to me. "You've been falling behind. Look at the amount of files on your desk," she leaned in running her fingers across their open edges. "I understand it's been busy, but that doesn't mean you neglect your work." She ridiculed in a sweet tone undercut with daggers. Her temple pulsed rapidly behind her thin ghostly white skin. At that moment I felt a deep hatred for her consume me. Considering I had undergone two accidents in less than twenty four hours and my body felt like a Mac truck had hit it repeatedly, I thought I was making great progress.

I painted on my best smile and used my most syrupy voice, "Samantha, can I help you?"

"Since you've been so interested in that woman," she said in a buttery voice, planting her skinny ass on my desk, "I thought you would want to know they think they've identified her. A police report had been filed and the description matched. The police are on their way now to talk with the sheriff. "

"Thanks, I appreciate that bit of information. The files really aren't as bad as they look. I've organized them and now I've started putting them away."

"Uhh… make sure you have that completed before you go home and..." her eyes radiating a hole inside my noggin, "Why are you walking like a geriatric mishap today?"

Embarrassed to say since I'd always been very graceful, but with no choice I responded. "I tripped yesterday at the hospital."

"You," she almost chuckled, "Maybe you should get your ears checked, your equilibrium could be off." She had never been my favorite person but I had never hated her either. At this moment, it became official - yup, I hated her. I couldn't believe my own thoughts stemming from an unknown part of my temporal lobe.

That night, the clouds rolled back in, only this time they brought rain. The rain gently tapped against my window, leaving trails of water flowing like tiny streams against the glass. I tossed, turned and at some point fell into a sleep.

Inside my dream, the wind gently blew and the rain flowed vertically to it. The sky was grey with thick clouds. The sun was hidden somewhere behind them. It was neither day nor night, just grey all around. There were no people or buildings and the ground was neither solid nor liquid, but in between; squishy, like walking on a wet sponge. In the distance somewhere I heard a voice singing. I couldn't tell from which direction it came. I stood still attempting to discern where it was originating from but it sounded more like it was coming from all around. I walked in no particular direction trying to locate the source of the ballad. I wandered for what seemed like miles and still was no closer than before I began. It was like I was in the song, part of the song. I couldn't make out the words, but the melody carried a sleepy rhythmic beat. It made me feel good and forget the rain.

Water tendrils flowed down my body and my light gown was drenched and clinging. The song made me forget. Forget the rain, the clouds, and the grey all around. I wanted so much to find where the music was coming from but no matter how far I ran or walked or how far I traveled the song was still everywhere.

When I awoke, I felt different in a way that I didn't understand. The birds were chirping and the sun was pouring in my window. I could hear the normal sounds of the neighborhood, but something was changed. It was a feeling from somewhere down below in my gut. Puddles left in the holes within the sidewalk remained, and water collected in the drainage. The air smelled crisp like clean linen. Last night's shower had left its imprint forcing my knowledge that it existed. The weather had been teasing me for the past week, threatening thunderstorms. I heard its voice say *I'm here, you can't avoid me anymore.* My dream echoed inside me, *rain and a lullaby, rain and a lullaby.*

I went on to work, but couldn't fathom what rain and a lullaby had to do with me. The dream had seemed so real, maybe Samantha was onto something and I had a medical problem? I couldn't ignore any longer the bizarre reality that had become my life. The old *me* was slipping away and I was becoming someone or something else.

I found myself staring out the window at the exact spot the woman had run me over the day before. Why was she in such a hurry that she bumped into me and kept going? Why hadn't she even noticed that she left me sprawled on the sidewalk? She was looking in another direction, away from me. What was she looking at, or who? There was something off and vaguely familiar about the woman but what? I watched to see if she would again be there; looking down the street in the direction she had been running but of course she was gone. I pondered these questions over and over. A force from within me wrenched away and I needed the answers. They were important.

"Sunshine," I felt a tap on my shoulder, which startled and brought me back from wherever my mind had wandered off to. "I have some news."

Immediately, I shuffled some notes across my desk to look as though I was busy and cover up my daydreaming, "Joe, I got everything filed. Oh, and I typed up that letter for you." I handed him an envelope.

"Thanks, I have some information about our nameless woman."

"That's great!" I exclaimed.

"Her name is Eilida. She lives with a roommate, Sage, in Chesterville, she filed the missing person report." He read from his notes and continued on with the story. "They were supposed to meet up with friends, but she never showed. As the night grew longer, the weather started to pick up and became too dangerous to drive in. She had assumed that Eilida decided to stay home because of the weather. Eilida had always been scared of storms and refused to drive in bad weather. Sage was not surprised or worried when she didn't show and spent the weekend with her boyfriend returning home the following Monday after work but Eilida wasn't there."

He flipped to the next page of his notes, then he continued using the same nondescript tone. "At first that didn't seem odd as their paths didn't always cross daily because of their differing schedules. They are both college students and work part time jobs." Joe cleared his throat while flipping to the next page in his notepad before he continued, "Eilida's car was also gone so she assumed nothing odd. Sometimes she would drive up to her parents and stay there a few days, after a week Sage had begun to worry. She tried calling her but got her voicemail. She left messages. This went on for a couple of days and Sage became worried. She called Eilida's parents." Thumbing his notepad over again, he continued. "They said she wasn't there. In fact, they hadn't been home but vacationing. They hadn't heard from her at all. That is when Sage made the police report." I clung to every word. Ideas flashed through my mind.

Curious, I asked, "Do we have a picture?"

"I'll get back to you on that."

At five minutes to five, Joe got back to me. "Here is the article. We'll be running it in tomorrow's edition." The copy he handed me was full color and it contained a picture. She had dark brown hair with natural ringlets that flowed around her face and across her chest. Her eyes looked black as the darkest night and her smile was gentle. She was very beautiful in her own way; maybe more unique in appearance than beautiful, exotic even. She had a face that couldn't easily be forgotten. The picture started to ring bells and I had seen her before. Suddenly, I felt a "sick" coming on. Tomorrow, I would be making a trip to Chesterville.

Sick Day

Eilida

A steady rhythmic beep, beep, beep filled my ears. I was alone in a dark room. How long had I been here, days, maybe months? A table to my right held dozens of flowers and stuffed toys. A row of shelves behind my feet held dozens more. A small worn monkey stared at me from beneath a bouquet of daisies. The beeping stemmed from a machine with a blue line that pulsed in a familiar pattern. It was a heart monitor and the wires that left it were attached on the other end to my chest. A neighbor of the beeping machine, the IV, was holding up a bag of cloudy liquid flowing into tubes that connected to holes in my arms. I couldn't remember what had happened or what brought me to this hospital bed. I had a few broken images of disfigured faces and sluggish voices. I can see that I'm on a bed but my body feels like its floating. Nothing, I can feel nothing.

A nurse strolled in whistling "When the saints go marching in".

"Well, how are you today?" Her face was bright and cheerful with dimples that accentuated her round cheeks when she smiled. "Looking good," she said as she checked my vitals and meshed the IV bag. Taking notes on a tablet, "I'll be back in about an hour to change that. Keep up the good work." Then, she was gone. I didn't get a chance to ask, why am I here?

Sunshine

Never in all the time that I had worked for the paper could I ever remember taking a sick day. I kind of figured it was about time and my body was in excruciating pain. I downed two ibuprofen tablets with a full glass of milk. The pain was still present, but curtailed to a dull ache. I set the GPS in my car and followed the computer animated voice. Turn left and follow for three miles, make a right onto Water Crescent Lane. The mechanical voice droned on but I found my way to Chesterville. It was a quiet little town nestled into the valley of Mount Wilde. Houses dotted the mountainside and trees filled the landscape.

A small community college sat five and three quarter miles outside of town. I had decided to start there. At this point I wasn't sure what I was looking for or why I was there except an external force compelled it. The parking lot was shaped like an L around the small school. A large brick building with the word, Admissions, sat to the far left of the parking lot and a few other smaller buildings were scattered about. I walked, following a sidewalk path that led to the back of the school. There was a smaller path with a walking bridge over River Freedom. I wasn't done yet surveying the school so I turned around and strolled through the buildings. A flyer caught my eye *Three Down, at Gino's* and in smaller letters underneath *Fire Roasted Pizza, Friday May 8th at 9 p.m.* I folded it neatly and tucked it away inside my purse. The date seemed important since Eilida went missing that weekend, in fact that night. Students toiled around the halls, chatting, snacking, and studying.

I headed back towards the river and the bridge. The view was dramatic and colors flowed from all angles stemming from the flowers. Larger boulders and smaller rocks accented the trail along the river. I was glad that I had found a pair of jeans. My closet was full of skirts, businessy jackets, vests, and blouses. I had to rummage through my dresser and found only one pair of jeans and a single T-shirt. My shoe selection was equally irritating, but I managed to find a pair of sneakers. I would really have to work on my clothes selection when I returned.

"E, wait up," called a voice. *Me?* I was the only person out here. I turned my head to see a young man jogging towards me. His chocolate hair flapped behind him in jumbled waves. He must be mistaken. I continued on.

His footsteps quickening at my heels, I wasn't sure whether to run or wait for him. Maybe he knew her? Alongside me now, "E what's up with the hair?" He was tall and thin but not gangly. With his left hand, he brushed a large flap of waves out of his eyes. He was more than vaguely familiar and I knew him.

"Jay," I uttered which surprised even me. *How did I know his name?* My hair has always been blond but I decided to play along, "I'm trying something different."

A dimple lit up his left cheek with a wide smile displaying his very straight teeth as he said, "Never imagined you as a blondie. Missed you in Chem... I got the notes if you want to meet up later?"

"Yeah, okay where at?"

"Gino's where else? Sometimes, you are one strange girl." He pecked my cheek and ran off backwards shouting, "About four thirty, got another class now," pointing to the invisible watch on his wrist.

Talk about weird - that was one of the strangest situations ever. *Who is E?* I must be her doppelganger, I surmised. They do say after all, that *everyone has a twin*. I found mine and was extremely interested in knowing more about her. The pain was beginning to return and the bumpy path along the river only stressed my soreness more.

My biggest question at the moment was how did I know him? Can brain tumors make a person telepathic? I really needed to get my head checked. Ambiguous recollections of being here before registered inside my brain, but the pangs in my buttocks and legs won out and I headed back to my car.

I checked my phone. The time was twenty six after one and I had missed a call from Jerry. *Shit, shit, shit!* I had forgotten to call him and tell him I wouldn't be at work. He had probably stopped by for lunch. I texted him a quick message *Sorry, I am still sore from the fall took day off be home later.*

I took a left out of the parking lot and followed it until I came across Temptation Drive and turned right. This road followed the mountain upwards. I hadn't thought about where I was going until I came across Eclipse Lane. My driving had been mechanical as if I had followed this path hundreds of times before.

There were three houses on this road and I was frighteningly close to the top of Mount Wilde. To my left was a small brick house with the number fifteen hanging on the brick close to the front door. Directly across the street was another brick house, number eighteen, with yellow police crime scene tape surrounding it. At the end of the street was a wooden A-frame. I parked my car along the street and surveyed the area. *What happened? Why the crime scene tape?*

Curiosity got the best of me and I exited my car and staggered towards the taped house. Suddenly my legs became jellylike again and the house in front of me started shifting. The bottom of the house relocated itself from the roof and then continued rearranging. Snowy static filled the air around me. I felt as though I was walking into an old horror movie. Closer to the house my legs became more difficult to control and I almost fell. Steadying myself, I rested against the home and clutching each brick walked around it. In front of my eyes flashed blood, in flowing streams. Catching my breath and fighting to stay afoot, I stopped. A crack of lightning beamed from the sky, leaving a hole in the ground. Smoke elevated from it. Within seconds, I was covered in rain, drenched, unsteady, and cold, I half stumbled, half crawled back towards my car.

What did I do?

Eilida

Most of my ribs are broken and bruised and there are several fractures in my legs and arms. Stitches cover my body, feeling like millions of needles poking at my skin. The doctors say I'm lucky that I didn't break my neck or back. They also say that I slipped down a mountain side during a harsh thunderstorm but I can't remember a thing. My mind is a complete blank as if nothing existed until waking up here in this hospital. I have so many questions. Who am I? Where do I live? Why did I fall? What was I doing on that mountain in the first place? Do I have family, friends, people who care? What will I do and where will I go when they release me? There's nobody to answer these questions so my brain spins in circles.

My hospital stay has not been altogether horrible. People have sent me flowers with stuffed toys; teddy bears, fluffy dogs, but mostly bears - and someone sent me a monkey; he's my favorite. His fur is no longer fluffy and soft but matted and coarse; his black beady eyes hang from their sockets by a thread; like a child's favorite play toy. Something about him brings memories to just below the surface of my mottled brain, just out of reach. Flowers cover nearly every square inch of my cubicle disguising the hospital smell.

A young girl, Jasmine, visits me daily and reads stories to me, changing the inflection of her voice for each character, breathing life into their cardboard souls. She's about fifteen, with skin the color of brown velvet and eyes the color of dark chocolate. For every gift I've received she has read every card except the monkey because he came as is, no card. When I woke up, he was here staring at me with his dangling black dot eyes.

I can't remember my dreams, but when I awake, I'm covered in sweat and my heart monitor is beeping wildly. One night, I woke up with tears rolling down my cheeks. I figure maybe my mind is trying to piece together everything that happened. It's sorting through what I need to know and what I don't want to know; putting all the 'don't need to knows' in the trash. Several scenarios play continuously through my subconscious explaining why I might have been on that mountain.

My favorite is the bank robbing synopsis. It goes something like this: I robbed a bank a few counties over, stealing a few cool million. In order to make a clean getaway, I had previously staked out a home abreast the mountain top to use to stash the money and lay low. In the basement, I had removed a few boards from the wall and made a secret compartment. Inside I hid my money. As soon as the heat died down, my plan was to take the money and slip out of the country undetected. I incurred my injuries when my partner, who I was double crossing, found me. We fought over the money.

Finally, I lied and told him I dug a hole in the forest and stashed it there. I took him to the hole which of course didn't exist. He handed me the shovel and forced me to start digging, but I was cleverer than he. I dug for a bit and when he wasn't watching took the shovel and whacked him upside the head. I pushed his body into the hole and ran back to the house for the money. The rain was coming down in wicked torrents and I slipped and fell, rolling down the mountain, and ending up in this hospital. My goal when I leave here is to find that house, grab my money and invest it in some offshore accounts. Then I'll fly to Belize where I will live wealthy and happy for the rest of my life. Yes, an unlikely story, but it could happen.

Sunshine

I started the car up and got off the mountain as quickly as I could, careening around the corners, sliding through torrents of flooding water. I nearly lost control of my car, and spun around. Luckily, it made a complete 360 and stayed on the road, stopping within inches of a huge tree. I steadied my grip on the wheel and took a minute to take several deep breaths.

I grabbed my phone which had flown off my passenger side seat and lay on the floor beneath. Jerry had called again. I ignored his calls as I didn't want to talk with him now. I would do that later tonight. The time read five after four. It was almost time to meet up with Jay, so I GPS'd Gino's pizza, and checked my mirrors. Calmer, and convinced no one else was on the road, I pulled back into the driving lane with my GPS to guide me.

Gino's was a dive. It smelled of grease and the stage barely looked big enough to hold an entire band, maybe the drummer. Jay waved at me from a corner booth with a beer in his hand. His saggy T-shirt and wild hair made him look at home in this type of establishment.

He handed me a beer and said, "I ordered your fave."

"Thanks," I wasn't sure what my favorite was. Pizza has never been a food I indulged in.

"Oh yeah," he said as he foraged through his backpack finally pulling out a binder that looked as though it had seen finer days. The plastic was ripped from the corners and the binding seemed to be missing. He pulled out a few pieces of paper that were written with extreme neatness, not what I would have expected to come out of his scraggly binder, and handed them to me.

"Thanks," I managed. About to take the papers, suddenly I remembered my engagement ring which I quickly took off and jammed it into my still damp pocket. Most likely E wasn't engaged. I took the papers from him. He had excellent handwriting and the organization was impeccable. "Did you write this?"

"Uh, yeah. I always give you my notes and you copy 'em."

Well duh, I thought, *because you know me but I don't know you.*

"Yeah, yeah, yeah I'm sorry I seem out of sorts. I got hit by a flash flood driving from the mountain."

His eyes grew twice their normal size as he said, "It was wicked out there. I took some pics." He pulled a phone out of his baggy pants and glided his finger over the surface. Sliding closer to me he said, "Take a look. This one is vicious." He pointed towards a picture of the river. The water rushed through it completely covering the rocks I had seen earlier in the day.

I had drunk three beers by the time the pizza arrived. The beer was disgusting, but something about it quenched my thirst and took the edge off my frazzled nerves.

"Do you have any pictures of us?"

Puzzled, he asked, "Us?"

My curious mind wanted to know if I really looked that much like *E*, "Friend pictures?"

His puzzled look disappearing, he said, "Let's have a look." Once again, fumbling with his phone he placed it on the table in front of us and scrolled through.

"Wait, wait, is that me?" I asked.

"Who else would it be? You've been blond - what like twenty four hours and airheadedness has already caught up to you?" He barely got the words out as he was laughing too hard. I took my fingers and made the picture larger moving it around the screen as I studied it. The picture looked just like me except the hair was darker.

"Can you send me this picture?"

"Sure."

"Wait, I have a new number." I said, trying to keep the edge out of my voice. I recited as he started to punch the number into his phone.

"You really are blond." He said, shaking his head. Now I wore the puzzled look?

"That's been your number."

"Oh, uh, yeah, too much beer," I droned questionably. I'm sure he thought me an idiot. We finished eating the pizza, and apparently my favorite was mushroom, Italian sausage and pineapple. The spice from the sausage was set off by the sweetness of the pineapple and I found my taste buds fancied it.

Suddenly, feeling the beer and music, I started dancing to the beat. I grabbed his hand and pulled him to the dance floor with me. I felt so alive, young, and free. My hair bobbed in all directions and my body just wouldn't quit. The pain I felt earlier had vanished. Caught up in a slow dance, I wrapped my arms around him.

What I did next I truly can't explain. It was one of my new strange sudden urges. I planted my lips on his. His tongue met mine and the next thing I knew I was in his bed where I shouldn't have been although he felt so good pressed up against me, our bodies flowing and meshing together. Soon after he fell asleep and I gently lifted myself out of his bed and grabbed my stuff. I fumbled towards the door, putting my clothes on and left.

I couldn't believe what I had done. I was a soon to be married woman. The guilt ate away at me the entire drive home. Jerry was perfect and he had a great job. We would have an impeccable life together, how could I throw all that away to some young kid who didn't even know the real me? I had to keep this secret.

Uh Oh

Eilida

Sometimes, I have this sort of image in my head. A memory maybe, but I don't really know; it could just be residual effects from one of my frightening and forgetful dreams or the medications they keep pumping me with. The image is of a palm tree swaying gently in a breeze, but that's it. I have tried putting all my brain energy into the image, but nope, all I get is a gently swaying palm tree.

Sometimes I focus on the palm tree while looking at my monkey and they come together, the monkey and the palm tree. I imagine him in the palm tree cracking open coconuts and drinking the succulent milk. Sometimes I think that is why I have chosen Central America as my get away choice. Monkeys, palm trees and Central America just seem to fit together.

A new image begins to form within the cobwebs of my mind; it fights vehemently to take hold. Through the fuzziness the form of a person struggles to exist, but instantaneously vanishes, leaving a warm, melty feeling inside me. I focus once more, and I can see a smile with straight teeth. Teeth that make me want to climb my tongue inside and feel around. I explore further and can taste sweetness and spice at the same time. Music plays in the background.

"It seems you have a visitor." Says one of the nurses and poof my impression dissipates.

Besides the hospital staff and Jasmine the only other visitors have been the police. They ask about my progress. How soon will I be able to speak to them? One even talked to me, Detective Henderson. He recalled what he'd been able to piece together of my accident but none of it rang a bell. It was a complete blank so I tuned him out and thought about the monkey swaying from the palm tree eating coconuts happily. That officer hasn't been back in to speak with me since but he talks with the hospital staff every day.

My visitor today is a young woman by the name of Sage. She is beautiful, like an angel with strawberry blond hair that bounces as she walks and eyes so green they resemble emeralds. *Do I know her?* I can't remember. She is the epitome of gorgeous. The woman every other woman is jealous of. I think I'd remember her if I knew her. She calls me Eilida. Well, that is a start at least. Now I know my name. She says we are housemates and best friends. I listen to her talk. She seems kind but I don't trust her.

According to her, we live on the other side of the mountain from where I was found, in my grandmother's house. She brought in pictures. The pictures are of the two of us together, some with other people, some are pictures of mountain scenery. She shows me a picture of a man and a woman that she says are my parents, but they don't look like my parents. OK, not that I can remember my parents, but I picture them in my mind differently.

I see my mother with hair black as a raven and eyes deep as the ocean and my father was strong and muscular with broad shoulders. The people she calls my parents look… well… different. She, my Mother, has mousy brown hair with subtle streaks of grey and bright round brown eyes. My Father has black hair with streaks of white and he's definitely balding on top. He has a beer gut not a six pack. Maybe they used to look the way my mind's eye perceives them but over time grew to look like the pictures. It's a long shot but maybe. Sage seems very kind; however, I'm just not sure I can trust her.

Going back to my whole bank robbing theory, she could be the partner I whacked with a shovel. Maybe she's trying to find where the money is? Like I would tell her, crazier things have happened. *Why can't I remember?* I know the whole bank robbery thing is a fantasy and my life was probably pretty boring and my parents probably are those people in the picture and Sage is probably telling the truth, but for now all I

have is fantasy because I don't remember
reality…

Sunshine

When I reached my apartment, Jerry was
inside waiting for me. "Where have you been?
You can't return my calls?" Part of me felt
guilt from my illicit actions only a couple
short hours ago. The other part of me felt like
I was being scolded by my parents for staying
out past curfew. His words awoke a feeling
inside me; not unlike a lioness waiting to free
itself from a cage.

"Really! I was a grown woman last time I
checked. What? Now I have to get your
approval?" I squawked. His eyes went from
angry to sad within seconds. I quickly spied
the missing ring on my finger; glad he hadn't
noticed, I muffed around in my pocket
searching for its whereabouts. A wave of
panic forced its way over me when I didn't
immediately feel it. Relief washed over me
when I felt the points on the rock, and knew
it was there. He continued his speech, while I
nonchalantly, from the confines of my pocket,
wiggled the ring back on my finger.

"No, I was worried. You took the day off
and never called to let me know. All day I've
been calling you. You responded once with a
text?"

My heart softened. I would be worried, too, if I was in his shoes. "You're right. I should have called. I'm sorry." I moaned, feeling his sadness.

"Can we sit?" he asked. I heard my shower and bed calling, but I knew we needed to talk, better sooner than later. I took a seat on my lazy boy. I didn't want him close enough to smell another man on me.

He occupied the edge of the couch closest to me. Taking my hands, he said, "You don't have to sit so far away."

"It was closest."

Placing his hand over mine, "I'm worried about you, not only the events of today, but... the last couple days something has been different about you. Look at you. You're wearing jeans frazzled and muddy on the ends; your shoes are caked with it and your hair is unkempt." He smoothed over my knotted blond strings. "Is this pre-wedding jitters?"

All that came to mind was *I you love and betrayed you*. Gaining a hold on myself, I replied, "No, I ached still from my fall at the hospital. Joe had given me some information on the young lady so I took the day off, drove to her town, and looked around. I got caught in a rain storm that's why I look this way. Really, I'm OK and yes, I want to marry you. Right now, I'm tired and in need of a shower and sleep." I gave him a peck on the cheek and escorted him to the door. He was obviously more than confused. I decided that conversation would have to wait for another day.

OMG!

I thought. *He was right I'd been off lately.* Everything in my life was changing around me and I was changing with it. I needed to get back into my normal routine, find my lost piece of tranquility. For the rest of the week, I minded my *Ps and Qs* and did my best to forget my lusty moments with Jay.

Friday afternoon, Jerry and I went shopping. I felt I needed to make up time with Jerry since I did the unspeakable with another person, so I asked him to come. My closet was dismal and I had ruined my only pair of jeans and sneakers. I wanted comfy clothes.

Everything I found he gritted his teeth and said, "This would look better," holding up some preppy dress, skirt, or blouse. He was driving me nuts!

I wanted to shout but instead in my most pleasant voice said, "I'm not here for work clothes. I need practical everyday jeans, T-shirts, sneakers, and maybe some sweat pants".

"You've never worn any of that before. I'm not used to your new style." My new style… arghhh… it wasn't for him to agree. It was my body and I would dress however I wanted. I could feel my rebellious side rearing its nasty head as I grabbed a few pairs of jeans off the rack and stomped into the dressing room. I liked the fit because they made my ass poke out. I felt hot and sexy. I purposely didn't show him what they looked like. Taking my new sizzling hot jeans, I marched to the counter and laid them out before the cashier.

"I got this, if it's important to you then I'm buying," he offered. Confused, I looked up at him and his face was the picture of sincerity. The rest of the evening went much the same way.

At dinner that night, my phone started beeping; glancing at the display, I saw it was Jay. I hadn't heard from him at all since that night. He sent two messages with attachments. While I fiddled with my phone Jerry cleared his throat in an effort to hint at me to put it away and pay attention to him. Looking up, I replied, "It will just be a minute, its work related." *Bullshit, it wasn't work, but he would never know.* I downloaded the attachment to the first message and it was the one he had of *E* that I had seen the other night.

The waiter arrived with pad and pencil, "Are you ready?" He took our orders and I excused myself to the restroom. Inside the stall I took another look at the photo. I was sober now and I knew the face, well kind of. I dug around in my purse pulling out two pieces of folded paper. The first was the article about the woman. I placed the picture of the hospital girl next to the one staring at me on my phone. I eyeballed them closely and the only difference I could see was the newspaper girl's hair was in spiral ringlets and in Jay's her hair was straight. Bells went off inside me with the realization that E was *E as in Eilida.* Next, I pulled out my driver's license and sat it down in between the pictures. I didn't have to study the picture. It looked like the other two with one exception, my blond hair.

Suddenly, the room closed around me and I felt as though I was being suffocated. Blackness promised to creep inside of me, however I fought to stay here in the now. My torso fell hard against the wall as I brought my head between my knees and took long, hard, deep breaths. After a few minutes I was back. The room looked normal and the blackness was gone. The other paper still lay folded beside the pictures. Unable to look at them, I turned my head and grabbed for it. With my fingers I uncurled it and with my eyes, still careful not to see the pics, scanned the writing, Jay's chemistry notes. I had to get these back to him.

I carried myself back to the table. Jerry looked at me with his eyebrows furled and asked, "Everything alright? You look like you've seen a ghost."

I knew I must have looked bewildered. I felt like a ghost or an echo of someone else. "It's fine, really."

His wrinkled forehead and uplifted eyebrows told me that he didn't believe me. I was barely able to touch my dinner.

Wedding Cake

Jerry's mom and my bridesmaids came down for the weekend. The plan was to go cake and gown shopping with friends, an all-girl weekend. Priscilla and Kaila joined us. They were my longest known friends that I still kept in touch with and because of that, they were my bridesmaids. Priscilla was tall. Her shoulder length chestnut brown hair was extremely thick. Kaila had long legs, a perfect ten body, and hair that fell in silken twirls across her back.

This weekend was a much needed break from Jerry. It was also a welcome distraction from Jay. We must have checked out every bakery and tasted a sample of every wedding cake. I wanted something simple but soft, moist with whipped frosting that wouldn't be too heavy. After frequenting just about every bakery we found what I felt was the perfect cake, vanilla with a lemon whipped topping. The cake was three tiers high with a frosting bouquet of flowers on top and vines flowed down the sides.

We completed the day by stopping for dinner at Manella's. Where we ordered a large salad and lasagna. This restaurant was great because their large dishes were made to feed four. We parted ways with full bellies.

The following day was set aside for dress shopping. My soon to be mother-in-law had made an appointment at Memories for twelve thirty. It was nearly ten by the time we set out. We met for brunch and had bagels and coffee. I was really starting to feel excited and little butterflies fluttered inside me.

Memories was a high class wedding boutique. I was starting to feel more like the self that had been lost. I chose a beautiful magnolia white dress with a delicate plunging neckline, a tight waistline and a hemline that stopped just short of my ankles. It truly was a perfect fit. Not many alterations would have to be done. The bridesmaid's dresses were a light shade of yellow, like a delicate tulip opening up.

At the florist we decided on matching yellow roses and baby's breath, along with lemon colored carnations with coral tips. By the end of the day we were tired and famished.

I had a fantastic time but couldn't shake the feeling that I was being followed. It was after dinner while heading back to the car that I saw her. All I could see was her flowing dark hair and small frame as she stood alone not twenty feet from me. Her chin was angled downwards and her face was hidden from my view but she was the same woman I had seen before. I was sure of that. I was so intent on watching her and identifying where I'd seen her before that I tripped when the heel of my shoe hit a pothole in the parking lot. I was wearing one of my new sexy pairs of jeans so I didn't get hurt but a small rip had formed in the knee of the fabric.

"Sunshine, are you alright?" asked Kaila as she offered her hand and helped me up.

"Thanks, I've been such a klutz lately," this was an honest and true statement on my behalf.

I looked back in the direction of the woman but she was gone. Priscilla drove and I rode shotgun. We laughed and joked most of the way home. I had been talking with Kaila and Jerry's mom when I turned forward. It happened so quickly that there was no time to think so I reacted.

I let out a blood curdling scream, "Stop!" She, the woman from the parking lot, was in front of the car with black tendrils of hair streaming across her face, making it impossible to see it. My wail made everyone jump and Priscilla slammed on the brakes. The car skidded and we all hurtled forward as far as our seat belts would allow. I hopped out of the car and ran around. She was gone. I was sure we were going to hit her.

Priscilla jumped out of the car. "What? Nothing is here!" She was right, but something had been here. At this moment, I felt insane but I had seen her, directly in front of the car. Not wanting to sound as crazy as I felt, I made up a story. "I saw a deer. It was huge and heading towards the headlights. You know they are attracted to the light."

"I didn't see a deer. I saw nothing but open road."

Jerry's mom stepped out of the car too and interjected herself into the conversation. "Sunshine, I'm sure you saw something but its dark. Are you sure it was a deer?"

Kaila got out of the car, as well. I was surrounded by them and I felt as big as a peanut.

"Would you have rather I didn't scream? Would you rather be pulling windshield glass out of your foreheads with a dead deer straggled through the windshield?" I screamed at them. The air was silent and I could read their faces. They didn't believe me.

It was Priscilla who broke the silence and finally spoke, "It's late and I'm tired, maybe there was a deer, maybe there wasn't." She put her arm around me and continued, "You're my friend and I'm thankful we are all safe."

As we piled back into the car and headed home I unmistakably heard thunder crackle in the distance. I did my best to keep up appearances but my thoughts were elsewhere. Rain, a storm, the woman; does it always rain after I see her? This was the first time that thought had engaged my brain. I jumbled through all the trash that had piled up in my cerebrum, digging for my first encounter with her. The restaurant, ping, I could hear the bells going off inside. It rained for a few minutes afterward. Then I was knocked over by a mysterious woman in a black hoodie. Was it her? Going back to the old adage which states that it's better to be safe than sorry, I assumed it had been. The clouds had moved in and then back out, dropping no rain until later that night. I'd dreamt of being in the rain and an alluring voice had sung some type of lullaby. It came from all around me. I was part of it but saw nothing but grey everywhere.

I was startled out of my reflections when a *CRACKLE, SPLAT* hit the ground just missing our vehicle. The lightning lit up the night sky in a sharp streak beaming down into the ground beside us. Then, came the rain. Not a gentle summer storm but torrents of water which threatened to engulf us. Priscilla fought to keep control of the car. The water was flowing so fast and strong that the little coupe felt as if it would get swept away. Then the rain stopped as quickly as it had initiated and the flood waters receded.

In the privacy of my bed, I thought about all the quirky occurrences that had invaded my life; the faceless woman, the rains, the quick but forceful storm tonight and in

Chesterville. This brought my attention to the little hospital of horrors. What happened there followed me to Chesterville and happened again and my betrayal with Jay. The pictures too!

They say that brain injuries can alter a person's brain waves, make things possible that might not be possible otherwise; like seeing ghosts. Is this cryptic woman a ghost? My imagination ran wild but it made sense. The only other options were traumatic brain injury or a tumor. Paranormal activity made so much sense.

Outside my windows, the wind growled and groaned and the deluge was back. It came down in cycles, downpour and calm, downpour and calm. My need for slumber overcame the chill that traced up and down my spine.

My sleep returned me to the grey and mushy, spongy ground that sank under my feet. The song was much closer this time. More audible, I could tell it was a woman's voice. Through the thick air, I was able to make out movement and a shadow.

Instead of following the voice I pursued the shadow. I continued my journey towards it. I felt if I could just reach it the ferocious storm outside would subside and I would be out of harm's way. The rain falling faster and harder, I was sopping and my visibility was more and more limited. Through the rivulets invading my eyes the shadow appeared to be large and oval. I grew closer and closer finally able to identify the soft form of a face.

The image before me was fuzzy but I could see outlines of the eyes and a nose but not the mouth. Under the nose was still something indefinable. Soaked to the bone I continued. Somewhere inside my soul I had heard the lullaby before. A memory flooded back in disjointed pieces; being held and rocked, a storm and a man.

Suddenly, to my right, he came out of the fog towards me. "There you are," he said. His voice sent a sharp pang echoing through me. As a reaction, I ran. My feet driving hard into the sinking ground beneath them. The rain turned to blood and a wooden chest, the kind a woman would use to preserve her wedding dress in, materialized before me. Scrambling to reach it and close the lid I jolted awoke.

Tears covered my face. Outside, the lightning illuminated the sky and water pounded my window. The dream had unleashed a very real terror inside me. My body shivered and I yanked the covers up under my chin and curled myself into a ball. I could hear my own heartbeat.

After what seemed like an eternity I remembered I wasn't alone, my soon to be mother-in-law was in the extra room. At the moment I wanted nothing more than a mother's comforting loving arms. I rushed out of bed to find her shaken from sleep as well. Together we went to the living room and sat on the couch. Not a word was said, but soon we both fell asleep in each other's arms.

Eilida

Fever had consumed me and I shivered under my covers with sweat pouring out of every crevasse. A three tier wedding cake and bridesmaids danced around in my head. A hideous rainstorm nearly washed us off the road. Without warning, I was no longer in a car with friends driving in a ferocious squall but I was walking towards a proverbial melody following a dismal apparition.

A man coalesced before me, his face ambiguous, and his voice that of demon spawn. It mocked my existence. My feet took hold and pounded the saturated earth until a wooden chest manifested before my eyes, it represented safety from the beast.

Oh my head! Static reverberated against the walls of my skull leaving lacerations across the folds of my brain. A familiar warm feeling squeezed my hand. It was that of my mother. I recognized her face from the pictures but the warmth of her hand was native to my existence. She was indeed my mother and comfort washed over me.

Opportunity

Sunshine

The events and my crazy dream over the weekend lingered inside me. I spent most of the day contemplating what this poltergeist could possibly want from me. My research had told me they appear when a person is most vulnerable to them and usually they have something important to communicate. Has my aura changed and left me vulnerable? Did it go from pink to silver indicating I have psychic abilities or has it changed to black indicating sickness hence my imaginary brain tumor? I felt a strong pull to get back to Chesterville… to Jay and unraveling the strangeness surrounding me. An internal voice said all the answers could be found there. My own connections were being severed and retied to someone else's memories.

Tuesday, I found my excuse to return to Chesterville when I overheard Francis, the reporter working the Eilida case, take a personal cell call. His face grew soft and visibly upset as he entertained a phone conversation with his mother. All I heard was, "I'll be there, mom." Immediately, I knew it was about his father. His dad had had a series of medical problems the past several months. Francis dropped his phone back in his pocket as he slipped into Joe's office. I positioned myself within ear shot of Joe's office and strained my hearing to listen in.

"My father is ill again. The doctors don't know if he's going to pull through this time. My mom is alone at the hospital so I'm flying up tonight. I'm all she has if Dad passes."

Joe replied, "I'm sorry. Take care of your parents. I'll find someone else to go or I'll do it myself."

I took that as my opportunity to jump in. Casually, I walked in on the last part of the conversation, making like I had a question for Joe. I used my most sorrowful and sweetest voice as I said, "I didn't mean to overhear and I'm really sorry Francis. I'd like to help," then, I paused and switched to my thoughtful, suggestive voice, and continued, "Maybe... I could go... you know... to Chesterville."

"You," replied Joe abruptly. "I had no idea you were interested in reporting."

"I haven't thought about it but I know the ropes." *Lies, lies, lies, well not completely.*

Joe twisted his face in thought, then, he responded, "I don't know, Sunshine."

Francis interjected at this point and offered, "I think she can do this. I'll give her my notes and catch her up on my leads."

"Hmm..." said Joe, as he swished his thin lips side to side. "Ok, I'm going to trust you with this one." Swiveling his greying baldish head to me and narrowing his eyes then moving his gaze to Francis, he declared, "Get to work. You have a lot to do and little time!"

Elated, I gave Joe a huge hug and whispered, "Thanks." I hadn't noticed until then that he had ear whiskers; grey hair growing out of his ears.

The job didn't seem too difficult. The piece he had been working on was a tribute to Eilida. The job entailed taking pictures and interviewing her friends, family, co-workers, and college professors. I could do that.

Before Francis left, we went back to Joe and gave him the details of our plan. "Good plan. Francis, her parents and roommate have been at the hospital here?" It was more of a question than a statement.

"Yes, sir," he responded.

"Sunshine, I'll do the interviews here. Get yourself to Chesterville. I want this ready by the weekend," he said, wearing his most stern expression. I was feeling excited. I had never thought about working in the field. Now, the opportunity had arisen and I already had an in that Joe didn't know about, Jay.

I dashed back to my apartment and packed professional clothes for the interviews and some of my new sexy, comfy clothes for Jay and undercover work. I wrapped my hair in a tight twisted bun and went heavy on the makeup. I usually wore it light, the pictures I'd seen of Eilida she didn't wear any, so heavy was good. I was still wearing my gored skirt and silk blouse from work and checking myself over in the mirror I no longer looked much like her.

I texted Jerry *leaving town for work call you later <3 u.* Then, I texted Jay, *Got your notes meet me.* My libido was overly excited and yearned to be with him again.

It was a quarter past one when I pulled into the parking lot at Freedom Hotel. I assumed named after the river. The "hotel" wasn't much of one. The sign blinked the letters Free_ _m _otel. It was a brick structure, a traditional Chesterville style, and single story. There looked to be about thirty rooms that formed an H shape with the parking lot straddled between. I was given room twenty nine which was located at the top of an arm of the H. Jay had texted back *meet me at my place. 7 study session.* Seven was good, it gave me time to do some work first.

I had decided to start with the college. Francis had given me a list of Eilida's classes and professors along with their office hours. I started with Dr. Gumbatz, her creative writing professor, as Francis had an interview already set up with her. He didn't leave her office number so I went to the admissions office. The lady at the desk was young and greeted me with a warm smile saying, "Can I help you?"

"I believe so," I pulled out my media ID as Joe had instructed me to do. "I'm here to see a Dr. Gumbatz could you direct me to her office?"

"Sure, you'll follow the hall," she pointed towards a long hall to my right, "When you get to the end turn left and she will be in the first office to your right."

"Thanks," I responded.

I traced her directions and found the office, and Dr. Gumbatz sitting inside at her desk with a stack of papers in front of her that she was engaged in reading. She wore glasses that sat on the edge of her beak-like nose. I assumed she must be reading student work.

I knocked on the door. She lifted her head in my direction, "Yes?" A puzzled expression crossed her face and she shifted her eyes to something on the wall above the door which I assumed must have been a clock because she suddenly said, "Oh oh, I'm sorry… are you from the paper? Please come in."

She stood, shook my hand and gestured me in. She was short in stature, no more than four feet, extremely thin with course thick black-grey hair which she wore in a pixie.

Removing a stack of papers and relocating them to a shelf she said, "Take a seat, please. You have to excuse me, its finals and I have stories to read and grade." She gestured to the piles lying everywhere around her office.

"I'm Sunshine," I said, introducing myself. "You had spoken with Francis but he was unable to make it. We are doing a piece on Eilida Riley." I didn't want to give her too much so I stopped there.

She slipped the glasses off her beak and sat them on her confused desk while she said, "Sweet girl, this is my second semester with her. She took my college composition class last spring, and now creative writing. She has a wonderful imagination but there is a benevolent darkness in all her work." *Benevolent darkness?* I couldn't help but ponder what she meant.

"How?" I asked.

She rummaged through some files and pulled out one labeled E. Riley. Inside, she flipped through some papers and withdrew a couple. "It's best you read for yourself," she handed me a couple pieces. I scanned over them. The first I read was a short story about a jealous wife who plots to kill her husband but is double crossed by her husband's nurse. The other, a poem that read:

'Twas the Night Before Death
'Twas the night before death, when all through the trees,

Not a creature was stirring, not even a flea.

The fireflies buzzed around houses with flare,

In hopes that the Grim Reaper soon wouldn't be there.

Little Delilah all nestled and snug in her bed,

While visions of a bloody knife circled her head.

Mamma in her red scarf and dad in his,

Had just been sliced by a razor sharp knife.

When outside the house arose such a clamor,

Delilah sprang from her bed to hide from the slasher.

Scarlet flowed from around the familiar bed,

Giving way to a flood of crimson and red.

When what to her fearful eyes should appear,

But evil incarnate with a blood tipped dagger.

Shifting and searching not willing to leave,

Little Delilah stayed hidden it must be the beast.

As I read Eilida's words, the name *Delilah*, in a sinister voice, resonated inside my head and a stinging bout of shivers crept across my spine. I wasn't sure dark was the word I would use to describe her writing, although they gave me a lot of insight to who Eilida is.

"Her dream is to be a reporter not unlike you. Currently, she freelances a column at the Chesterville Star. It's called..." She searched her brain for another few seconds then in a triumphant recollection said, "Dear Delilah. It's an advice column."

After reading her poem and short story, I wasn't sure an advice column was the most appropriate placement for her writing. Horror screen plays seemed more up her alley. Next on my list was interviews with co-workers. I made a mental note to read some of her advice.

Dr. Gumbatz went on verbally drawing me a great visual of Eilida's character, a young, possibly deeply deranged, woman. Before leaving, I asked her, "May I keep a copy?"

She flashed me the evil eye, which I found spooky that college professors could do every bit as manically as any grade school teacher. "I wouldn't usually, but something about you reminds me of her so I will make an exception but you can't print them," she said in a sudden hard-nosed tone.

This little woman could be a force to be reckoned with. Abruptly, my mind conjured an image of her karate filleting monsters three times her size. The intimidation I felt stung my soul.

"Thank you and I most certainly won't. Could you tell me which office I could find a…" I said flipping my notepad back to page one, "Dr. Jekal?" A chemistry teacher named Jekal. I found that a bit cliché.

"Towards the end of the hall," she moved over a stack of papers on her desk, "Number twenty three. It will be to your left," she said. I smiled and thanked her again. She went back to her grading before I had made my last step out of her office. If I was lucky, Jekal would be in his office.

Dr. Jekal's office door was closed. I wondered if that was because Hyde was present. Anticipation welled up in my belly over the thought, but I sucked it in and rapped softly on his door. It was returned with, "Door's open, come in." His voice sounded normal enough.

I cautiously entered and introduced myself, "Hi Dr. Jekal. I'm Sunshine from the Lyden Times. I was hoping you may have a few minutes to spare for a quick interview about one of your students."

His office had shelves of books strewn about haphazardly. A quick glance at their titles told me they were all chemistry and biology related. He was very tall and thin with short coils of hair that stood out randomly.

He wore a dress shirt half tucked in with two pens, one blue and the other black, behind a pocket protector. *Really, could he be any more stereotypical?* I wondered. I shook the thought out of my head.

His face seemed frazzled as he checked his watch. "I can come back another time if that would be better," I suggested.

"No, uh… sit, sit," he replied. His eyes blinked rapidly and his movements were robotic. "I have fifty three minutes before my next lecture. I can spare you twenty." He had it down to the minute? Can we say overly time-absorbed or maybe OCD.

Nonetheless, I responded in kind, "Thank you, we are doing a piece on Eilida Riley. Could you tell me what kind of student she is?"

He responded short and to the point, "She is an average student in chemistry." I could tell this would be like pulling teeth. Twenty minutes later, I had she is an average student, gets along well with her lab partner which I intuitively knew to be Jay and missed the last class which is unlike her. I felt like I was writing up a teacher conference log.

I checked my phone and it was nearly three o'clock. I had some time to kill before study group with Jay and used it at the public library to read some of Eilida's Dear Delilah articles. Most of them consisted of mundane trauma, from *I saw my best friend's husband at dinner with another woman* to *how can I get gum out of carpet?* Finally, one article stood out and it read:

Dear Delilah,

When I was ten a family tragedy separated my younger sister and I. She was only two. After years of searching I have recently learned her whereabouts. She is now married with three children. I want to get back in touch with her but I'm not sure what to say after all these years. Seeking your infinite wisdom, Ted.

What struck me was the infinite wisdom bit. It sounded smart-aleky and taunting. Her response was very professional and wise for someone of twenty three years of age.

Dear Ted,

Your caution in reuniting with her goes without saying. It is very likely she doesn't remember you, your parents, or the tragedy that separated you. Remembering you may also be a trigger to those memories, and you want to start out on the right foot in order to rebuild that relationship. On the other hand, you don't want to gain a new relationship under false pretenses. I suggest starting with a simple straight forward letter introducing yourself without highlighting how you became disunited. If she responds then you have a starting point. Be gentle and ease slowly into her life. Allow her to determine the flow of the relationship.

I printed the article and checked my phone again. It was five twenty three which meant Jerry would be getting off work. I went back to the hotel and called him. I told him my reason for being here and some of the information I had pieced together. I even read him the Dear Delilah article I had printed. His keen observation noticed something that I hadn't. In her response she mentions she may not remember *your parents* but he said nothing about *their parents* in his inquiry. He said a family tragedy, which could be a million other things besides the children both being separated from their parents. Was she reflecting on personal experience or was it conjecture on her behalf?

Eilida

My mother brushed my hair while Jasmine read me another story. Each brush stroke brought another emotional recollection into my memory. I was still unable to recall actual events and people in my life only the affection and love of my mother.

Jasmine finished reading the chapter and before she left my mother asked her, "Honey, will you grab that mirror for me?"

Jasmine responded, "Yes, ma'am," and she handed her an oval vanity mirror with a pearlized blue handle.

My mother put the mirror in front of my face and stated, "You see how beautiful you are and your hair has always had such graceful ringlets." Her voice changed from comforting to nostalgic, "When you were a baby, those ringlets were so tight they looked as though I pulled curlers right out of your hair. When they were brushed out, your hair fell to the end of your back but they would bounce back so quickly…" Her voice trailed off. She held the mirror to the side of my head opposite the stitches so I was unable to see them. The bruises in my face were now a slight yellow as they were mostly healed. Altogether, I thought I didn't look too bad for the severity of my accident but I wouldn't say I looked beautiful either.

Study Group

Sunshine

I pulled out a pair of store bought cutoffs with premade bleach stains and a purple tank with a built in bra out of my suitcase. The tank squeezed my boobs together and allowed a nice cleavage view. In front of the bathroom mirror I took off my makeup and pulled the pin holding up my hair. As it fell to my shoulders, it grew dark and I was no longer looking at me but Eilida. My heart moved into my throat and I staggered backwards and whispered, "Are you my ghost?"

Guardedly, I stepped back to the mirror and ran my finger across its surface. The mirror was solid and the reflection now my own. Shaking off the freakiness, I finished brushing my hair and gathered it into a high pony tail without the use of the mirror then slipped on my new flip flops. I felt comfortable and thought I looked great. I rubbed lip gloss across my lips and puckered. Not yet ready to look in the mirror again for fear of seeing the ghost, I hoped the gloss covered my lips. A sudden wetness crept between my legs as my mind lingered on Jay.

The sun was beginning its downward journey to the horizon. Trails of colors filled the sky giving me an unforgettable drive to Jay's. He lived on the second floor of a very ordinary looking building. It was brick like most other buildings in Chesterville and a staircase supporting a shaky wrought iron hand rail brought me to his door.

There were no potted plants or chairs outside, nothing that said I love my abode, but definitely said I'm a college science nerd. I knocked and when the door was opened a young man, not Jay, greeted me.

"What's up, E?" He put his hand in the air which I instinctively knew to high five.

I'm not sure if it would register as the oddest part of the day, since today had been riddled with peculiarity, but I knew his name and responded without thought. It was like my actions were being controlled by a hidden remote.

High fiving, I responded, "Ely," I drug the y sound out, "Ready to get my studying on."

Another young man picked me up from behind and twirled me through the air before setting me down in front of him. "Let me look at that hair."

He moved his head side to side and placed his hand in front of his mouth and then back to his side and responded, "It's not really you. It hides that inner gloom you wear so well."

Inner gloom, that's what would best describe what I was quickly finding out about Eilida. "Evie, Evie, Evie can't a girl try something new?" I asked. Knowing his name came as no surprise either.

Jay stepped into the room wearing nothing but a towel that hung below his waist and threatened to fall off baring the beauty underneath. His abs were chiseled which I hadn't noticed the other night. I bounded towards him and jumped, curling my arms around his neck and my legs around his waist. Still the towel lingered. He returned my affection with a kiss and put me down grabbing my arm as he pulled me towards the bedroom. Unable to control myself I pulled the towel off and it dropped to the floor.

With a beguiling look of surprise, he hoisted me over his shoulder like a gunny sack and said, "That's it! Look what you've done," and closed the door behind us. Plopping me onto the bed he drove himself into me hard and passionately.

We studied most of the night away and took a short break long enough to go to Taco Express for quesadillas and ultimate tacos loaded with cheese, peppers, beef, onions, sour cream and possibly a few other ingredients.

I felt a type of kinship towards Ely and Evie which put me in a quandary and I asked myself, *does Eilida have brothers or close cousins here?* I didn't think so, as they made no mention of any family that may link us, but it is a small town. I put myself into her place in my thoughts.

A bright light lurked behind the curtains and I pulled a pillow over my head realizing then that I was burrowed into the crook of Jay's arm. Instead of gathering my clothes and leaving, I dragged the covers over my head and went back to sleep.

Sometime later the smell of coffee aroused my olfactory sensors. The scent brought back memories and I envisioned a young raven haired woman holding a small baby in one hand and a coffee mug in the other. Softly she placed the coffee onto a table while holding the baby up to the window. They were looking outside watching two young boys and a man. The man had no shirt on and his skin was a deep shade of brown. His torso bearing carved muscles. Beyond them was a vast ocean. Slowly the figures faded and I knew I had remembered something important. A past that grappled with my present and for that short time I was Eilida.

I turned to find Jay missing. I jolted out of his bed with the sudden revelation and feeling of crushing loneliness and wandered to the living room where I found Jay and Evie talking. Scents of pancakes, eggs and bacon wafted through the air, teasing my taste buds.

I knew without a doubt, that Ely was cooking breakfast.

"You're still here?" questioned Evie in a mocking tone. It had been the first time ever that I spent the night in bed with Jay. *Eilida's first time…* A curious instinct that I knew that tidbit of information.

"Yes, I am. Is that so strange to you?" I asked.

He laughed and looked at Jay, "I think she's got a thing for you."

Eilida

Flashes of people filled my head but the quickness of the flashes made it difficult for my mind to understand. I fought to hold onto these memories as having any had become a commodity. I saw young boys with dark hair, a football and an ocean with a man… my father? No, not my father, I don't know, dark and handsome. Several quick bursts radiated behind my eyes. The water was deep and blue, sand everywhere. Laughter echoed around me and I was staring out a window watching them while being held up by loving female arms but not the motherly arms that held me now.

Sunshine

Luckily, I had thought to throw some extra clothes into my huge purse that I had bought the day I went shopping with Jerry. It was multipurpose and roomy. I took my own car to the college as I had begun to remember who I was and the reason for my being here. At the college, I scurried to class and for yet another unknown reason I knew exactly the room. Dr. Jekal sat at a table with a stack of tests beside him, and a copy of Current Chem held up to his face.

Each student took a test, sat down quietly and got to work. Afraid Jekal might recognize me from the previous day, I tousled my hair so waves fell across my forehead hiding my eyes. I kept my head down and swiftly grabbed a test. I took a seat towards the back and got to work. With confidence, I knew the majority of the answers and it wasn't the study session last night that triggered them. I had been surprised when studying last that I knew the material. I couldn't remember taking chemistry but my memories as of late had escaped me. Thinking hard I couldn't remember anything further than a couple weeks ago since the Monday I went to work and learned of a young woman, Eilida, who had tragically been found at the base of Mount Wilde.

The Chesterville Star

At the hotel, I showered and changed into a pin skirt, light blouse, and short kitten-heeled shoes. Taking in a deep breath and letting it out, I cautiously glanced into the mirror; no ghost. I let out a sigh of relief and began applying my makeup rather heavily and twisted my hair back into a bun again, leaving a few loose curls across my forehead. Pleased with my appearance, I hurried out the door to get to the Chesterville Star.

I was immediately greeted by a bubbly blond receptionist, her style in work attire much like my own. The office had partitions separating the "offices" and was painted a cream color. A few fake plants spotted the entrance and a coffee table neat as a pin stood to my right. It looked almost identical to my own office. I shook the thought from my head.

"How can I help you?" She asked.

I decided to forget the niceties and move into the meat of my visit, "Do you know an Eilida Riley? She does the Dear Delilah column here?"

She scrunched her pug little nose and drew her mouth into a poignant smile. "Of course, she only comes in once or twice a week but has been with us since she moved here a couple years ago. Her grandmother passed away and left her house to Eilida. She lives with a friend. Oh… what is her name?"

I interjected, "Sage."

"Yes, that's it!" Glee lit up her face from end to end.

Well, getting information from her would be easy. After listening to her bear Eilida's life story, at least the parts she knew, a young man walked in and placed a simple peck on her cheek. "Oh, Harry this is… uh… I don't believe I got your name. How rude of me talking away and we haven't been properly introduced. "I'm June," she said, as she shook my hand.

"I'm Sunshine," I responded, returning her shake.

"This is my fiancé, Harry." Harry had chestnut hair and bore a striking resemblance to someone I knew somewhere deep inside. She showed me her ring finger and displayed a huge rock that unmistakingly looked exactly like mine, down to the cut of the diamond. Suddenly, I felt dizzy and fought to keep myself upright.

A man of about forty strolled over to her. His jacket, tie, and slacks matched impeccably. He wore his hair slicked back and he was incredibly short, no more than an inch or two taller than me. I leaned my body into a chair seated opposite June's desk.

"You should be at lunch and I need you back in an hour sharp. I've got several items that need your assistance. Hurry, what are you waiting for?" He barked at June. He was a male version of Samantha.

Déjà vu, far too many coincidences. I had lived all this before.

"Yes sir. Oh and this is Sunshine. She's with…" He cut her off.

"And bring me back a cheese steak from Olley's, extra meat, peppers, and onions." I feared if she messed up his sandwich, he would chain her to a dungeon floor. She and Harry scurried out the door.

"Ian," said the male Samantha, introducing himself but not offering his hand as June had. His temple pulsed rapidly behind his thin skin much like Samantha's.

"Sunshine with the Lyden Times," I answered. At this point, I was ready to run from this vicious little man but I was here as a reporter and I didn't work for him. I had to remind myself of this throughout our short conversation. From June, I had learned many fascinating personality quirks about Eilida. From Ian, I had gotten close to zip. Dr. Jekal had been more personable than Ian.

As I approached my car, I could feel my purse vibrating from my cell. I reached in my purse to grab it and a small slip of paper fell out. I caught it just before it hit the ground. My phone was still in my hand and I dropped it back inside my purse and opened the small note. It had an address written on it, Fifteen Eclipse Lane. I repeated it a few times in my head, *Fifteen Eclipse Lane, Fifteen Eclipse Lane,* then, boom! I had it! The house on the mountain across the street from the crime scene! June must have slipped this inside my purse as she left. It had to be Eilida's address.

I called Jerry back on my way to Fifteen Eclipse Lane and we talked throughout most of my drive to the house. I knew no one would be home as Joe had mentioned her roommate Sage had been at the hospital. It would be easy to look around and get some pictures so long as my legs didn't go jellylike on me.

Fifteen Eclipse Lane

I hadn't forgotten the last time I was there but I wasn't going to let my fear encompass me either. Cautiously, I parked in her driveway and walked up to her house. My legs weren't jelly yet. I peeked inside. I couldn't see much, even when I sheltered the glass with my hand. The sun was too bright against my back. I took a look across the street and snapped a few photos. The house still wore the same crime scene tape it had last week. My curiosity wanted to know what had happened at that house but my job was Eilida.

I moved to the side of the house hoping to get a more shaded view when I tripped over a rock, sprawling forward. I was able to catch my fall but I had kicked the rock belly up. It contained a key. I loosened the key and tried the front door but no luck. So I traipsed around to the back, watching my steps as I went, I didn't need to reinjure my bum again. There was a back door, as I suspected, and when I wiggled the key in the lock the door opened up.

The walls were painted white with flowery six inch borders below the ceiling and the furnishings were mostly antique. I assumed they were her grandmother's, left to her with the house. I didn't feel as though I was invading her space; on the contrary, it felt like my own.

A heavy wooden cabinet sat to my left. I knew inside was a TV, an older model, tube style one. When I opened the doors the TV was staring me down. Beneath the TV was a series of drawers. Running my fingers down them, I opened the bottom one. Occupied inside were shoeboxes filled with pictures. I sat on the floor and milled through them.

A lot could be learned about a person through pictures. Eilida's parents' house, or at least, that is what was written on the back, had a very strong resemblance to Jerry's parents' home and her parent's bore a striking facsimile to his. He was an only child. At this point not much surprised me and I concluded it could only be another peculiar parallelism.

Upstairs were two bedrooms with a Jack and Jill bath between them. Instinctively, I knew which was hers. It was very tidy. An opened laptop sat on a roll top desk. I pushed the button and it started right up. A password box popped up on the screen and intuitively I typed the word Chloe. A Dear Delilah letter filled the screen, it said...

Dear Delilah,

This is Ted again. I want to thank you for your advice. I have been in touch with my sister. In fact, I will be meeting her and her family tonight. Thank you, Ted.

A follow up to the letter I had found and copied? It was dated May eighth. Swishing the date around my head a few times an epiphany struck me. May eighth was the night she had her accident. I closed that letter and worked through all the new ones giving them each a reply. When I was finished I submitted them all. Completing the activity was second nature although I had no idea why I did it except to say I felt compelled.

As I pranced down the stairs, I caught a glance out the front window. The sky had turned black with clouds and night quickly approached. From the corner of my eye I caught movement in the house across the street. A shadow passed in front of the window and then disappeared. My heart stopped for a split second and blood drenched the walls. Not the walls of the house across the street but another, the paint underneath baby blue. I held my eyes closed and counted to five, and when I reopened them all was normal and the sky outside was turning to dusk.

Eilida

My parents and Sage sat around my bed sharing stories and passing pictures back and forth. None of it set off any bells inside my head. My parents' home looked something like an older plantation home.

The monkey and the beach played softly around in my mind. I remembered them and the two little boys playing football, the tide rolling under their feet. Without warning, images invaded my mind and streaks of blood puddled a wooden floor and coated blue walls. A shadow danced across a window. The fragmented pictures left a sick wrenching in my gut. To rid the feeling I focused on the monkey who brought me an inner peace.

A nurse strolled in, "Visiting hours are up," She said as she tapped her watch. "Only one of you can spend the night. Who will it be tonight?"

My mother looked at Sage and placing her hand on Sage's hand said, "Sweetie, why don't you stay the night?"

A compassionate smile swept across Sage's face and she responded, "Thank you, Mrs. Riley."

My parents gathered their stuff and both leaned in giving me a kiss on opposite cheeks. "We'll see you tomorrow," said my father and gave me a wink.

When everybody had left, Sage climbed in bed beside me and whispered in my ear, "You're looking pretty good, you know. I'm going to call Jay tomorrow. I know how much you like him and it's obvious how he feels about you. Now is not the time to deny the relationship forming between the two of you." Jay, he must be my boyfriend? Is he one of the fragmented images that had passed through my more-full-of-holes-than-a-kitchen-sponge memory? She smoothed my hair, kissed my cheek and sang "All through the night". She had an amazing voice and before I knew it sleep had washed over me.

Sunshine

The bloody images that flashed through my mind creeped me out, goose pimples dotted my arms. I raced out of the house and jumped into my car, wasting no time peeling out of the driveway, switching the gear shift to drive I punched the gas leaving a dirt cloud behind me. At the base of the mountain, my heart finally regained its normal beat and my breathing became regular. I checked my phone at the hotel and it read seven seventeen and a message begged my attention. It was from Jay and read *Ginos at eight*. I responded *be there*.

One to the Head

He wasn't there when I arrived so I took a place at the bar. "What'll you have?" asked the bartender, a man average in stature with wooly hair and a gruff voice. His face was weather worn and a grizzly beard resembling a dead squirrel covered his chin. He had obviously not lived the easiest life.

I had never been much of a drinker, mostly an occasional glass of wine. Last week I had my first taste of beer. I was feeling adventurous tonight so I asked, "What type of shot would you suggest?"

"Sure you can handle that?" he said with a grim expression.

I responded honestly, "No, but I'd like it anyways. It's been a rough couple of days." That was an understatement as the last couple days had been beyond insane.

"You asked for it," he mumbled under his breath as he took a clear liquid, poured it into a shaker over some ice, and served it. I took it to the head in a single swallow nearly falling off my barstool as my throat and esophagus felt like a wildfire had engulfed them and I started gagging.

The bartender stayed close filling a glass with a carbonated beverage from a squeeze nozzle attached to a tube. Evidently, he had a good idea what my reaction would be and handed me the glass of fizzy liquid. "Wash it down with this." His eyes never left my face as if gagging wasn't enough. He then suggested, "Let me get you something I think you'll like." He poured a couple different liquors into the shaker along with a red syrupy liquid and shook for thirty seconds and put the concoction into a cocktail glass. He concluded the process with sugar around the rim and a couple of strawberry halves floating on top and handed it off to me.

"This is a first," said Jay's familiar voice.

"It is?" I was more than a little confused.

"You never beat me here," his eyes questioning my memory.

"Always a first," I said holding up my drink.

Gruffy the bartender, brought Jay a beer and looked me over again, "E?"

I guess I should know him since I'm obviously a regular. "Hey, fooled you." I said in hopes of saving some dignity. "You like it?" I spouted as I smiled big and bold, flipping my hair.

"You look like an entirely different person," he replied studying my hair as I placed my hand under my chin and cocked my head from side to side. "Think I like the natural color better." *Don't they always say that…?*

I pulled Jay's notes out from my purse, placed them on the table and said coyly, "I forgot to give these to you last night. I guess it doesn't matter anymore."

We both laughed and Jay's face lit up in an ear to ear smile. "You always keep them too long but I have a photographic memory so I never complain." Another one of those things I was supposed to know. I glimpsed a bashful smile his way.

"How do you think you fared on the test?" he questioned.

"I think I did alright. I passed I'm sure. You?" I responded.

"I aced it. The study sessions aren't really for my benefit."

He's a hot science nerd! I thought. What a turn on. I felt an overwhelming urge to pick his photographic memory so I asked, "You remember the day we met?"

He chuckled, "You spent the night and now you're getting sentimental on me. Is this a trick question?"

"No, I'm testing your memory," I replied.

Twisting his lips, he answered, "OK. You walked into chem. lab on day one with your hair pulled back in a ponytail and you were wearing a pair of running shoes. Your jeans looked like a bad washing machine mistake with bleach stains covering about fifty percent of them. You wore your favorite black hoodie, the one with the frazzled cuffs, zipped up to your neck." Wow! He was good. In my mind, the moment he described registered briefly.

We drank, danced, and ate my favorite pizza again. I'm guessing we didn't have frilly romantic dates since I was terrified of commitment or so it would seem since I, or Eilida, had been unable to stay the night with him, ever. I had the time of my life. No phantom or ghost or whatever she was came leaping at me. No thunderstorm worked on wiping me off the planet. I teased and played all night and we walked to his apartment about ten thirty. Ely was out but Evie was there watching a science fiction movie that entailed space ships, guns and aliens. I sat on the couch between the two as I, or E, had done many times before.

I decided to spend one more night with him. The next day, I would go home to Jerry and my life in Lyden and probably never see Jay again. I stole the chance and curled up next to his body and allowed the rhythmic hum of his heart beat to lull me to sleep.

What's with the Crime Scene Tape?

I woke early and slipped out the door, leaving Jay to ponder my actions. At the hotel, I showered and dressed. I had decided to find out more on the crime that happened at eighteen Eclipse Lane. I checked in with Joe reciting to him the strange characters and information I had learned with the exceptions being the extra bizarre reactions battling inside me. Suddenly feeling like a reporter, my gut told me to check out the house across from hers and I relayed this to Joe.

"Joe, the house across the street has crime scene tape across it. It seems too coincidental that something happened there and that she was found at the bottom of the mountain near the same time."

He replied, "You're sounding like a real reporter, you never leave a stone unturned. Check out the story. Detective Henderson has been working her case. I have talked with him on a few occasions. Try him."

"Thanks Joe."

"Sunshine, be careful. People in small towns don't always appreciate outside help and the perpetrator could be anyone."

I thought that through carefully and responded, "Thanks, I plan on coming back tonight and should be in tomorrow."

After we hung up, I gave a long thought to whether I wanted to use my media badge or act like a family member of Eilida's since I bore such a strong resemblance to her. I opted for using my media badge. Joe's warning resounded throughout my brain *the perpetrator could be anyone.*

I packed my bag and threw it into my trunk and dropped off my key at the front desk while I paid my bill. The police station was a long rectangular building with an oak tree on each side and heavy double glass doors. The receptionist or dispatcher, I think that's who it was, wasn't very friendly. She had stringy-bronzy hair with fuzzy ends like she had committed chemical suicide on it. She was skinny like a rail with heavy makeup that caked into the wrinkles of her face that moved when she talked resembling little worms. Her teeth were unevenly stained yellow and her fingernails were obviously acrylic and desperately needed a fill.

The little make-up-worms wiggled around as she asked, "What can I do ya for?"

"Is Detective Henderson in?" I asked. The phone began to ring and she answered, placing her index finger in front of me to gesture that she would be back in a moment. Her finger resembled an eagle talon.

Laying the phone back down on the receiver, she asked, "And ya are?"

Could she not say the word you? I wanted to ask her that but refrained. "I'm with the Lyden Times. I was sent here by our senior editor Joe McGinnis." I responded in as sweet a voice as I could muster.

She looked me over, answered another phone call and then she started pushing buttons. "Alright sweetie, when ya hear the beep, push the door. His office is down the hall and to the left of the break room."

Smiling, I motioned a thank you and disappeared through the door.

Detective Henderson was of average height and build. He carried a donut around the middle that fell over his pants which sagged because he had no butt. His hair was a classic comb over in an attempt to hide the obvious creeping baldness.

He greeted me warmly and then proceeded straight to the point. "I talked to Joe not more than thirty minutes ago. He says you're interested in the house across the street from Eilida Riley. Quite a thing that both appeared to have happened on the same night. I'm Detective Henderson." He said and shoved his hand at me in greeting.

"I'm Sunshine," I answered. That's when we shook hands. His palm was a little sweaty and the residue stuck to mine. I made a mental note to sanitize them when I reached my car. "Can you tell me what happened in that house?" I questioned, getting straight to the point myself.

He leaned back against his desk, "Sunshine, that's a different name. Are your parents hippies?" The unfortunate truth was I couldn't remember them; too many memories not my own had laid siege over mine.

I couldn't figure how who my parents were had anything at all to do with my question, so I politely answered, "I don't believe so, they just liked the name."

"Hmm… Maybe all that blond hair… but you're not here to talk about your name." He read my mind. "The case is still being investigated but what I can tell you is it was the goriest murder scene I've laid eyes on in my twenty five years on the force. The entire family is dead except for the little girl. She was left crying in the blood. It covered most every inch of their kitchen."

My stomach started to feel a bit queasy so I took a chair as he went on. "The entire family's necks were sliced." He gestured a quick hand movement across his neck. "Can't figure why he left the girl?"

Black threatened to close in around me. I closed my eyes and rivers of blood oozed across the wooden floor. Regaining control of what little composure I had left, I asked, "Is the kitchen floor wood?"

"How would you know that pretty lady?"

"It's a guess. Wood floors seem popular in this town. Detective, do you think Eilida's fall and those murders are related?" I fibbed slightly about the floors. I was afraid he'd think me crazy if I told him the truth.

"It was a rainy night - any evidence outside was washed away with the storm and she was found several miles downhill from that house."

"Several miles downhill you said. Her house is on the opposite side of the street - why would she be found downhill from their house?"

He scratched his cheek and continued, "Been asking myself that same question. You have a keen mind so I'm going give you a bone. Both parents were drugged before they were killed and the mother…" his voice trailed off, "She was raped."

He wanted me to give him the why, well that was easy, "Drugging the parents made them unable to fight back and raping the mom tells us it was definitely a man, a very deranged man."

"She wasn't just raped… it was done post mortem," he added. A voice mimicked inside my head taunting me, *De-li-lah*.

"Detective, what about her car?" I asked.

"That is a mystery. It was gone when her roommate came home that's why she took so long to file the report. It hasn't been found." He responded, folding his arms across his chest so they rested on his donut-middle.

"She didn't drive it that night, maybe the perp took it?" I was proud of my new found reporter-police lingo.

"Let's go for a drive," he suggested. I wasn't sure I wanted to, but again I had a mystery to solve and an article to write.

Eilida

Outside of my room, a commotion caught my attention. Well, commotion may be too strong a word but people, my people, stood in a huddle with my doctor. I had begun to think he was more of a figurehead as rarely did he do much. The nurses did it all. My heart went out to nurses everywhere.

"We can't put a time frame on it. Her CAT scan shows no abnormalities. Her vitals are stable and her wounds are healing extremely fast," said the doc. I read his lips and ad-libbed the words I was unsure of. He was talking about me so why not say it to my face? Why would my CAT scan reveal anything other than normal?

Jasmine strolled in my room. "Good afternoon, where were we? I found it," she said, taking a seat beside my bed, her fingers strolling through the book. I listened to her read and tuned out the doctor.

My head filled with visions as her words turned into a full length motion picture. The story was about a young woman who had tragically been abandoned at twelve. Now an adult, she searched for clues to who she was and who her parents were. The plot took many twists and turns and the closer she got to finding the answers the more questions she had. I related with her. I knew my family; they were right outside the door but I had no recollection of my life. I wanted answers too. I wanted my memory back.

No longer did I believe any of my crazy yet entertaining scenarios. Glimpses of my life bounced through my brain but nothing stuck. Was there such a thing as mental superglue?

Sage floated in, yes *floated*. She had more grace than anyone else. Today her strawberry blond hair was French braided against the back of her head and she wore tight jeans accentuating her long legs. Placing a kiss on my cheek and brushing her mouth towards my ear she whispered, "Love you, Lida." She called me Lida most of the time.

My parents entered my room, which was now exceedingly full, and they took a seat on the small couch. Jasmine paused from reading and said, "Good morning, Mr. and Mrs. Riley, Sage."

They returned her good morning and my mom said, "Please go on. I am as interested in the story as Eilida is." Curling her lips into a smile, she continued.

Shotgun Blasts

Sunshine

I got into the squad car opposite the Det. and we drove. I had never been inside one before that I could remember. His radio buzzed and made beeping sounds. Something that looked like a TV screen stuck out from the dash, turned in his direction. The car itself carried an odor of sweat. It wasn't pungent but distinctive.

He pulled up and stopped on a small graveled path alongside the river. He stepped out of the car and motioned me along, gesturing with his hand. I followed his lead and we walked parallel to the river, silence between us. The shallow river washed over boulders leaving grooves in the water that soon combined on the other side. From my vantage point, I could see a series of waterfalls that zig-zagged the mountain.

He pointed towards a monstrosity of a rock. "This is where she was found." I looked from the rock and up the mountain. Houses spotted the sides, but mostly all I saw was foliage.

"The mountain isn't very steep."

"It's old - been worn down. Someone called it in, a man. At first, we thought a local but we scoured the area, must have talked to everyone that lives in this region and nobody knows anything."

I deliberated that tidbit of info. "Could it have been him?" I asked.

"The perp? Could have been, but why would he call it in? It doesn't make sense. Most likely, it was some kid who didn't want to get caught partying. They come out here all the time."

That didn't make any sense to me so I asked, "Partying? It was storming that night, kids wouldn't be out here."

He chuckled, "Sure they would. Their parents own these houses along here." I took a look at the homes scattering the river. They were up on stilts to protect them from being flooded. Anyone inside them would have a good view of something or someone coming down the mountainside unless it was storming then their view would be obscured by rain and rushing waters.

He then took me up Mount Wilde to the house. I repeated inside my head *no jelly legs, no jelly legs*. We got out of the squad car, the radio squawking at us as we walked towards the house.

A deafening burst split the air around me and I hit the ground. A smile tugged at the corners of Det. Henderson's mouth as he offered me his hand. "You never heard a shotgun blast before?" With his available hand, he held his chin and continued,

"Happens all the time. When you live in these parts it becomes common place."

"Common place," I questioned him. "People randomly shooting firearms that echo through the trees, somebody could get hurt." Standing on both my legs now, I dusted off my pants.

Dumbfounded by his nonchalant attitude, I asked, "You don't worry about a stray bullet hitting an innocent person?"

His partial smile now a full-on smile, "Around here, no. Most these people own arsenals of permitted weapons and they know how to use them. They aren't amateurs like city folks."

Still perplexed, I continued my rant, "So, you just turn a blind eye to what they do? What could they be shooting at?"

"Squirrels, birds, snakes, tin cans, homemade targets, could be a lot of things," he explained. "You're asking the wrong questions. It wasn't a stray bullet that hit that young lady."

He then pointed to the A frame at the end of the street, "That couple, they have a homemade military grade shooting range in their back yard. You think she wasn't used to gunfire?" My mind envisioned two scruffy characters attired in camouflage. One slithering across the ground with a handgun and shooting down the targets which bounced back up riddled with bullet holes. The other scruffy character jumping from target to target blasting their heads.

The closer we walked to the entrance of the house the more unstable my legs became. I fought off the distorted visual effects. My body halted as he opened the door, "It's OK, it's been cleaned. I want to walk you through what we have pieced together." He responded, as if he was reading my mind.

I tried to will myself to walk through the door but I remained frozen in place. Then another blast spliced the air and I rushed to where he was standing.

"Haha, that got ya," he chuckled.

One slow cautious step at a time I entered the house. It was meticulously organized with humble furnishings. A couple crocheted throws covered each of the couches and their DVDs were alphabetized. Pictures in matching frames scattered the walls. Most of them were pictures of two little boys and a baby girl. They were a handsome family. "You said the little girl is alive. What happened to her?"

"We couldn't find any relatives on the mom's side and no one came forward. On the father's side a cousin of his came forward and took her in. They have a young boy about her age, nice couple. Everything checked out so she went with them. Hopefully she's too young to remember any of this and will grow up in a warm caring home." *A warm caring home, a warm caring home* I repeated as I looked around. The house gave me the creeps.

We walked into the kitchen and jagged glimpses of the blood bath laid open fire on my brain. The room became fragmented and then everything went black. "Honey, you OK?"

Through the fog inside my head I heard Det. Henderson's voice plead with me. As I opened my eyes the room was fuzzy and his round face came into view, floating above me.

"You fainted. Take deep breaths," he said as he gently raised my body off the ground.

"I fainted?" I muttered softly.

"Can you stand?" he asked.

"I think so," I said as he helped me up. He kept his arm around me as we walked outside to a deck.

He pulled out a chair with his free hand and carefully glided me into it saying, "You need fresh air then I'll take you back."

My eyes focused in on my surroundings. A breathtaking view unfolded before them. I could see clear down to a large boulder. "Is that it?" I said pointing downhill.

"What little lady?"

"The spot Eilida was found."

He craned his neck around and walked several paces towards it until I could barely see him through the brush. A young child's wail rebounded through my brain and voices whispered, *Sanny... mommy... there you are.* I shook to free them loose and off they scattered leaving me alone.

Scanning for Det. Henderson I caught sight of him tracing his foot path back up to me. "You got something. That's the spot alright. This is what I think, Eilida noticed something fishy that night and came over to check it out. She came around to the back." He motioned all this out as if he was an actor in a play.

Eilida

Sage lay in bed beside me flat on her back. Her hair sprawled behind her mingling with mine. "You remember the day we first met?" she asked. No, no I didn't. Not paying me any mind she continued, "We were in kindergarten. You were eyeing my Sunburst bar. The little yellow cupcakes with the smiling sun mixed into the frosting and the white filling in the middle. You had a Twinkle bar with the colorful coconut topping. I loved those things! So I really wanted your Twinkle bar and you wanted my Sunburst bar but you were too shy then to ask. I marched right up to you, sat down, and asked, 'You want to trade?' You smiled and handed me your Sunburst in exchange for my Twinkle. Then, I introduced myself, 'I'm Sage.'"

She made little girl voices as she told the story and I heard myself say, 'I'm Eilida'. She couldn't say Eilida. The ill part threw her and she called me Lida. She has stuck with it since, calling me Lida to this day. She wore a little green cotton eyelet sundress and I wore a little blue T-shirt with a bright yellow sun flower and my favorite pair of jeans. I remembered! I remembered her and a flood of memories with her washed over my brain.

Getting up she kissed my cheek and said, "I'll see you later cheeka-babe, I gotta run but someone else will be here soon to fill my void. I think you'll be pleased," and off she ran, blowing kisses my way as she flung her purse over her shoulder and exited the room.

I remembered the summer her parents got divorced and how she didn't want to go home. We were eleven and she spent almost the entire summer with us. The house was huge and we would sneak downstairs at night and turn on scary movies. We huddled together and buried our faces into one another's arms during the bloody parts. We thought we were sly and pulled the wool over my parents' eyes but they knew all along. I can't see my mother's face but I can hear her voice as she walked in and overheard us creating a horror story of our own. "It's those crazy movies you two watch at night. I wish someone would create parent filters for TV channels." My life hadn't been mundane. Sage had filled it with adventure and fun. She was like the sister I always wanted but never had.

I could hear my parents' voices outside my door but I couldn't make out what they were saying…

Mystery Solved

Sunshine

In a sort of trance, I stood up and finished Det. Henderson's words. He stood back and watched. Walking to the back door, I leaned my body flush against it and peered inside.

"She stood here, looked inside and saw the massacre; two boys lay across the floor, blood flowing from their necks." I walked to the spots where they had lain.

"The mother stripped of her pants, lying in the corner," I said, while I pointed to the corner between a hutch and small serving table.

"The father sat propped on this chair, his neck sliced from one end to the next; blood pooled on the floor around him," I said, grabbing hold of the chair.

"He left the bodies scattered about, sloppy. Something interrupted him? Eilida, she interrupted him, walking in and seeing the blood bath. Fear overcame her and she ran, stumbling in the rain eventually slipping on the wet dirt beneath her feet. He panicked and went out the front door, spotted her car. His vehicle safely hidden from the road, he took hers to cover it up and make it look unrelated." Suddenly, the entire crime was clear to me.

"You need to find her car. His DNA will be all over it. Did you scour the area for any hidden cars?" I barked as if I was the detective.

His eyebrows lifted high in surprise at my sudden recollection and he answered, "We searched this entire mountain and no vehicles not belonging here were found."

"Then he came back later and got it. How long had it been before this family's murder had been discovered?"

He scratched his head and responded, "About two days. It was one of the neighbor's dogs, the house at the end of the street. The dog got out of the house and ran right over here. The owners chased him up to this back deck and called it in."

"The people who have a firing range in their back yard? Jeez, it could have been them," I said.

"It wasn't them. They're a little odd but not murderers. The crime was done with a knife and they shoot guns. If it makes you feel better I checked out their alibi and they were at a gun show that weekend. It couldn't have been them."

The ride back to the station was silent. We had unraveled the mystery surrounding Eilida but a bigger question remained *who murdered this innocent family?* Before I left I gave

Det. Henderson my phone number and asked, "If anything turns up, any new evidence, please call."

"Sure will, little lady. You just helped me solve half my mystery." He waved as I pulled out and began my journey home. Music poured softly from the radio as I drove home singing along to every tune attempting to rid my mind momentarily of the day's events. My phone buzzed against the seat beside me. It was Jerry, "Hey," I answered.

"How was your day?" he asked.

"We solved the mystery," I narrated all the details to him and finished with, "I can't wait to be home. Will you be there?"

"I am at your place right now." I had already slipped my engagement ring back onto my finger and flicked it in front of me as I drove. Jay was fun, but I had said goodbye in my own way. I wasn't Eilida. Living in her world was a fantasy place full of dark corners and lingering beasts. Jerry was my man and best friend; I couldn't wait to be married to him. By the light of the moon in the privacy of my car I had made the decision to devote myself fully to him.

Jerry

I walked through my door and Jerry greeted me by wrapping his arms around me and holding me close. It felt good to be home. At nearly ten p.m., we snuggled together and talked until we fell asleep.

His alarm woke us when it started beeping. He sprung off the couch, "I need to go. Lunch?"

Everything was back to normal, back to how it should be, "Yeah, love you," and I blew him a kiss.

The sun was beginning to peek over the horizon. Now that summer vacation was here the children weren't out yet but joggers and dog walkers spotted the sidewalk. I was glad the sun was back. I dressed for work in a one piece knit dress and slid my feet into a cute pair of wedge-heeled sandals. I had my information for Joe but I wasn't a journalist. I had done the dirty work so someone else could take the credit.

I gave Joe my meticulously written notes and he was disappointed that I had decided not to write the article saying, "You made an A-plus detective. I saw another side to you,

Sunshine. It's a shame but I'm glad to have you and that delicious coffee back."

"Thanks Joe, it was fun but it's not me. That house…" I hesitated, "It scared me. No wonder she was in such a hurry. I would have probably done the very same thing with the same results if it was me walking in on that gory mess. How can a person so carelessly take the lives of four innocent people?" I asked.

A sober expression washed across his face as he said, "There are all types of sick people out there. I've been in this business a long time."

For lunch, Jerry and I stopped in at a little bistro around the corner from the paper. It was like old times. I was remembering old times which made it even sweeter. His mom had sent some designs for wedding invitations and we looked them over, finally settling on a lemon chiffon with raised gold lettering. We made a list of people to invite and decided to allow a plus one. Everything was falling into place and our wedding was only a short time away.

The weekend flowed seamlessly. Saturday, we drove to Memories to get the alterations on my dress completed and stopped for dinner and a late night movie on the way home.

The movie was about a young man who lost his wife during a freak storm which caused their yacht to wreck. He's found washed up on the shore of a private island. The inhabitants sent him back home. Beside himself with grief and unable to let go, he sees her everywhere. For years he searches and uses up his entire wealth in efforts of finding her. Finally at the end of his rope after a life time of chasing her ghost, he gives up and becomes a recluse. It is then, sitting alone in a bar when she walks through the door. He thinks his eyes have deceived him but they haven't. She has no recollection of him as she had sustained a major blow to the head during the ship wreck. The story ends with him winning over her heart once again. I cried. It was a beautiful and touching story.

I thought of Eilida and I wondered if she would regain her memory? I had relented to make another hospital visit. If I could handle the goriest crime scene Det. Henderson had ever seen then I could handle the little hospital of horrors, but not this weekend.

Sunday, we had an appointment with the pastor we had chosen for our ceremony. He had a friendly face with crow's feet around his eyes that wrinkled up when he smiled. His salt and pepper hair was cut short. "Good afternoon," he said shaking our hands and guiding us to two throne sized chairs. They made me feel incredibly small and I sat towards the edge of my seat so I could touch the ground.

He talked to us about the divinity of marriage; being monogamous and true to your spouse. Jay came to mind and how wonderful it had felt to be with him even under false conditions. I felt a steady stream of guilt course through my veins. It wasn't simply my unfaithfulness to Jerry but I had willingly and foolishly deceived Jay.

The air around me became stuffy and I excused myself, allowing Jerry and the pastor to wrap up the session. In the fresh air, I inhaled deeply, allowing the oxygen to overwhelm my lungs.

We finished the evening by cooking dinner together. We baked pork chops and steamed green beans that we covered with a butter sauce along with a loaf of French bread that I cut into thin slices. Jerry popped the cork on a bottle of Merlot. The cork went flying high into the air and fell somewhere near my curtain overlooking the street. We both laughed and then I went searching for the lost cork while he poured the wine.

"I found it!" I hollered at Jerry. When I stood up my apparition availed itself again. She was standing just behind the street light across from my apartment. *No, no, no I solved it. She's gone.*

My thoughts battled each other and from a far off fog I heard a familiar voice, *"Sunshine, you ready?"* Ready for what? *What or who was coming?* Subconsciously I responded, *Bring it on.*

Zooming back into the here and now I picked up the cork, threw it in the trash, and downed the glass of wine Jerry had waiting on the table for me.

"Thirsty?" questioned Jerry, his eyebrows furrowed in disappointment.

Rather than responding I took a seat at the table and motioned for him to join me.

After he left I caught myself staring out the window but she, my ghost, was gone. Maybe my mind was playing dirty little tricks on me and she was nothing more than a figment of my imagination.

More Sneaking Around

Eilida

By late afternoon, the visitor Sage had promised, Jay, came to see me. My mother was by my side. He strolled in dressed up, well for Jay he was. He had on a pair of khaki colored shorts that hung to his knees, a pair of leather flip flops, and a collared shirt. In his hands he had a small bouquet of flowers. A smile overwhelmed his face upon seeing me, displaying his flawless teeth, followed by a look of concern.

He set the bouquet down and introduced himself to my mother. "I'm Jay; a good friend of E's, no wait… Eilida's."

My mother smiled at his faux pas and gave him a hug. "I'm Mrs. Riley; Eilida's mother." Then, she whispered something inaudible to me, and they stepped outside the door. Jay had appeared in many of my recent dreams and had even been the star of a couple. My memories of him were tied to those of Sage.

Sunshine

The following week, I worked up the nerve to visit the hospital once again. It was after work and the hospital didn't look so menacing. My legs didn't jelly up on me but I wasn't sure about the elevator. *Face your fears, face your fears* I chanted silently. I closed my eyes and pushed the button. Swish, the doors opened before me. The elevator was empty. Taking a deep breath I stepped one foot in and then the other and nothing happened. I pressed the number three button and the doors closed behind me. *Breathe, breathe, face your fears* I chanted to myself.

When the doors opened up on floor three a tall, thin man with wispy hair was waiting to get on, and I was clutching the handrail for dear life. He looked at me, and with a gentle voice said, "It's OK now." His words resounded against my consciousness. *It's OK now.* Did he mean the elevator? Did I look that scared? I peered behind me, straining my neck as the doors began to close and he was gone.

When I got to her room, I stopped at the doorway. She was not alone. A drop dead gorgeous woman was lying in bed beside her. She had to be none other than the infamous Sage. The toilet flushed and out walked a more than familiar figure, Jay. He took a seat next to her bed. Quickly, I flung my body behind the door, and pressed it against the wall behind me. What am I going to do? I can't let him see me. If he's here then he knows I'm a fake. *Get control of yourself, Sunshine!*

I swiftly walked past the nurses' station. There had to be another elevator around here somewhere.

I heard Jay's voice, "You want something?" She responded but I couldn't make out her words. There was a snack machine ahead of me to my right. He must be headed there. *Think Sunshine, think.* I spotted a door that read *Supplies Employees Only.* I looked in both directions to make sure nobody spotted me and slipped into the closet. Inside was a smorgasbord of linens, including uniforms for the orderlies. I changed into an orderly uniform and headed back to her room. This was about the craziest thing I had ever done. She was alone and sleeping.

I realized that I had never actually seen her in person. I had been her, and seen pictures of her but now we were in the same room together. I padded across the room tenderly towards her as I didn't want to wake her up. Her body didn't look as bad as I had expected. I crept closer, moving at a turtle's pace towards her. A heart machine beeped steadily, rhythmically beside her bed, *beep, beep, beep, beep* it repeated. An IV stand holding a bag of cloudy fluid rested near the heart monitor. The fluid steadily dropped from the bag into a tube that connected to her arm. Moving closer still until I was staring into her face. She looked identical to me, identical! She was me and I was her!

Taking a step back and almost tripping, I couldn't believe my own eyes. The noise I made didn't faze her. She looked like sleeping beauty. I stepped closer again and slowly brought my finger to her arm. A shock of static electricity bolted through me and her eyes opened for a split second.

On the other end of the bed was her chart. I needed to see it. I rushed over and scanned it for something that was legible, something I could understand but it was mostly medical jargon. Her birthday sprung out at me, besides her name it was the only thing I understood in her entire chart, April 5th, 1990. This had to be more than coincidence. Two people can't possibly look identical and share the same birthday without somehow being related.

Astounded, I crept backwards until my legs bumped into a chair, my body slumped into it, the chart dropped to the floor beside my feet. So many questions flooded through every crevasse and fold of my brain.

I stood up and took her hand in mine; the electrical impulses had a heyday inside me. "It's OK now", I whispered into her ear. The very same words the tall elevator man had said to me. Her eyes flashed open again and stared straight into mine.

Eilida

An electrifying jolt pulsed through my body. I fluttered my lids and a blond me was staring back at me whispering, "It's OK now". For that split second, my entire memory overwhelmed my brain but then the connection was severed and all my memories receded to their hiding places.

Sunshine

I couldn't hold on any longer and when I let go her eyes shut again. From the hallway I heard Jay and Sage. I lowered my head and picked up the fallen chart placing it back into its slot. They entered the room and walked right past me. I kept my head lowered and slunk past them. I reached the hallway and found the linen closet that I had stashed my clothes and purse in. After changing, I stole down the stairs like a phantom and went home.

My mind attempted to make sense of the situation. I researched twins and twin connections even when separated at birth, head trauma and twins. I found hundreds of stories about twins who could feel each other's pain who were reunited later in life. I sifted through the hogwash and blubbery tales.

Nothing, absolutely nothing explained how I was able to see her thoughts and remember her memories. I wrapped my hands around my face and slipped off the couch to the floor with my legs straddled in front of me and pulled my thoughts together. The ghost I've been seeing is Eilida, I'm now sure of that, but she's not dead. I knew her boyfriend and fell for him even though I had never met him. I understood chemistry which I haven't taken beyond high school and took her final exam. I saw the entire sickening slaughter of her neighbors but hadn't stepped a foot in that house until a few days ago.

Instead of twins, I cross referenced telepathy and head trauma. I found an article written by a Dr. Reisen. She had extensive Doctorates including metaphysics and parapsychology. Head trauma can be a very serious occurrence. A person can gain psychic abilities such as but not limited to telepathy, clairvoyance, E.S.P., clairaudience, telekinesis and the list continued. *My psychic ability* I.E. my gut instinct, said because of our twin connection she had been able to communicate with me telepathically and possibly astrally project herself into my body without the knowledge that she's doing it.

She had the head trauma but we share identical DNA which has made me a candid audience. I clicked the link that said contact and a page popped up showing an address about an hour away in Hatters Park. I wrote down the number and address.

View from the Inside

At work, I called Dr. Reisen's office. Her secretary was kind enough to schedule me an appointment for the following afternoon. Mentally, I worked out what questions I would ask her. I also considered, within reason, what I would be willing to accept. I had always thought of psychic stuff as loony.

Jerry came by after work and I felt it was time to fill him in on some of the gaps. I waited until we had prepared dinner and ate. I knew what I had to say made me sound like a lunatic and I didn't want him to choke or slice his hand while preparing food.

I approached with caution, "Jerry, I love you," my eyes pleaded for his understanding, "I need your opinion on something." I searched his face for understanding. "Recently, I have seen this image, a person; she even knocked me over one day. At first, I didn't pay attention. Then, I thought maybe I had a brain tumor. I even contemplated that I was seeing a ghost."

Jerry firmly replied, "I think, honey that you have been working too hard. You spent last week in Chesterville where you met some strange characters and found out some disturbing news about a horrible murder. You were a reporter for a couple days and chose not to write up what you had. You gave that to Joe." He searched my eyes. "You've been on the computer trying to find information haven't you?" He asked.

"Yes, I have..." I chose to be somewhat honest, hoping for his support.

Without allowing me to finish he interjected, "There is a lot of false information out there. It's most likely a coincidence that you keep seeing this person. The story about Eilida Riley has been boggling your mind since the day you heard about it. Maybe your mind is looking for her so you notice her now when before you never did; like if I told you I want a red sports car, you would probably start seeing them everywhere, right?"

So much for support! Jerry was twisting my thoughts with male trickery. "Not exactly, I started seeing this woman right away, but it's more than that. How did I know the entire gruesome crime scene? She's in my head."

"In your head?" he questioned, raising one eyebrow higher than the other.

I had decided to appeal to another side of him. "Have you noticed anything different about me lately?"

"Since you've returned from Chesterville, no. You've been very normal," he said matter-of-factly.

"Before my trip?"

His eyes rolled to the top as they did when he was deep in thought. "OK yeah, you fell at the hospital, made a trip out of town without telling me, ate Chinese food without chopsticks, and have a whole new taste in clothing."

There we go; he finally got it out. "You see, you've noticed it too."

Something else suddenly struck me and maybe it meant nothing but since I was on a roll I blurted it out. "Remember that first night I came home from Chesterville alone." He started to speak but I cut him off. "Don't speak; allow me to finish. I had gone to her house, Eilida's, but I didn't know then that it was hers. I was driving and before I knew it, I was there. My legs turned to mush and the scene in front of me shifted dimensions or something. It was like watching a TV with bad reception. Then lightning hit the ground beside me. It came within inches of me along with a massive rain storm. I made it to my car and off the mountain. That's not the first time the rains have come when I remember her thoughts or see her. It's sporadic but it happens."

He contemplated everything I told him, then chuckling softly he said, "People don't control weather and just because it doesn't rain around my Sunshine, doesn't mean that it doesn't rain. When I was a kid it used to rain all the time but weather patterns change sometimes. We are just getting rain again." If he couldn't accept these little tidbits, how would he accept my twin theory?

We looked out the window to a clear night sky. Stars twinkled above the distant homes. In an effort to comfort me he said, "You see how clear the sky is tonight? There isn't even a cloud and tomorrow will be another perfect day."

Watching the stars glow brought me back to his parents' house and the fireflies. Her house, in my mind I saw her catching fireflies with another young girl, Sage. They were laughing and giggling. How could I tell him this? My eyes drifted to the tree across the street where I had seen her before. "Jerry… there, over there under the oak tree. You see her? That's her!" She was back. He had to believe me now. I couldn't make an entire person appear.

"Yes, I see something, could be a person under the oak tree. I have an idea maybe this person is lost, let's go outside and check, maybe talk with the person. I'm sure that it is just someone who is lost or maybe waiting for a friend." Jerry replied to ease my mind but he didn't actually see anything under the oak tree.

I went along with his blind scenario. "Maybe, OK, I'm not scared… and you are probably right." I wondered, *do all men have a paranormal block or just Jerry?*

We headed out the door hand in hand. To get to the street we had to go down a flight of steps. When we opened the front door, she, of course, wasn't there.

"She's gone but she was right there." I pointed in the direction of the tree.

"Her ride probably picked her up," he said.

Whatever, he didn't believe me even when she was standing no more than twenty feet away. "Maybe, I don't know or I'm losing my mind?" I stated.

He placed his hands on my shoulders and looked into my eyes. "Honey, no you're not. Your mind is just playing tricks on you." *Was he that blind, really?* He was most definitely in denial.

I shuddered from the sudden cool breeze and said, "It's going to rain. Look at the sky; remember how clear it was? We were just looking at the stars, and now they are fuzzy from the clouds. I told you they roll in after I see her. I can't control the weather."

Jerry, *Mr. Denial* and *I don't believe in paranormal science*, offered, "The clouds are off in the distance and will probably pass us by."

Hmm… Yeah right and pigs fly.

"Every time it rains at night I have the same strange dream. I'm walking in the rain, drenched, and a song is playing. I follow it but can't figure out where it's coming from. Last time I had the dream a chest came out of nowhere. It was a simple wooden chest. An ominous man appeared and was chasing me that is how I found the chest. I was ready to jump inside it when I awoke. Your mom was here. That was the weekend we went shopping with Priscilla and Kaila. Will you stay the night? I don't want to be alone."

Jerry held me tight and said, "For you, anything."

Can he feel the fear inside me? I wondered. We headed back into the building and even before the door had shut a crash of thunder wailed through the sky.

I jumped at the sound and apprehensively responded, "You heard that, it wasn't that far away. It's going to storm!" It was as loud as the shotgun burst I had heard at Eighteen Eclipse Lane. I barely completed my thought when lightning lit up the sky like fireworks.

"I think you're right, it sounds and looks like a storm. I have an early day tomorrow, let's hit the sack," he admitted I was right. Did my ears deceive me? This was a first; we crawled into my bed together.

He went right to sleep but I was too upset. We had never fought, ever. I had to take care of this before our wedding so it wouldn't interfere with our happiness. A barrage of thoughts circulated in my head, leaving me unable to sleep. I took a seat in my comfy reading chair. At some point I dozed off for a few minutes but was awoken by another thunder burst.

I peered out my window. She was back standing below it. The rain dripped off of her as she stood, her face angled towards the ground as always. *Who stands in the rain? If this is Eilida why can't I see her face?* Terror gripped me and I was scared, but I had been learning to face my fears. I threw on my sneakers which lay beside my bed and snuck out of the bedroom, careful not to wake Jerry. There was a flashlight I kept inside by the counter. I grabbed it and traipsed outside through the back door. She was gone again. I walked to her exact spot, where small foot impressions were left in the ground.

I asked the air around me, "Who are you? How can I help you?" The air didn't respond.

In the safety of my bedroom, I changed from my wet clothes into dry ones and jumped into bed curling up next to Jerry. His heartbeat lulled me to sleep.

Within minutes I had fallen asleep and entered dreamland. The rain came down stronger now. Instead of squalls flowing in and out, it was steady.

My clothes and body were thoroughly soaked but I could now clearly see the face and hear the song, a lullaby. The face was a beautiful young woman with raven black hair and eyes that were pools of blue. As I walked closer, it became evident that she was holding a baby. The child had curls of wild brown hair spiraling around her head. She was no more than a couple years old and sleeping. From within I felt an obligation - no; more a force to continue. It wasn't a choice. The woman laid the baby down gently and very quietly walked out through the door.

The walls of the house suddenly closed in around me and I was inside the house, inside the baby's room. Outside the window the rain persevered. The winds were strong and there were redbud trees that blew sideways from the strength of the wind. There was a stuffed monkey inside the crib with the baby but no other toys. The room had a rocking chair turned toward the window, a small dresser, a large basket with a few toys in the corner, and the crib. The curtains and bedding were white with a print made of tropical flowers. The walls were a pale yellow and a mural of a palm tree with cute bouncing monkeys was displayed on the wall opposite the crib.

I padded across the floor to the doorway to follow the woman whom I assumed was her mother. When I reached the doorway, I could hear other voices. I strained in an attempt to make out their words, but couldn't. They sounded muffled, although I could tell one voice was her, the mother, and the other two were male. I pushed the door open and followed the sounds into the hallway. Outside, the wind whipped ferociously against the house.

My steps deliberate, I advanced through the hallway and entered what appeared to be the living room. Seated on the sofa was the baby's mother and I assumed the father. Her raven hair flowed across her chest. The father was muscular, very well defined and cut like a carved statue. His shoulders were broad and protective. His hair was short and curly. Tangles the color of mahogany fell across his forehead and around his ears. In a chair across from them was another man. Chills scrambled up and down my body and my heart raced faster than a dog at the track. Taking in deep breaths, I brought my body back to normal.

He was short with a glowing bald head. Even though he was sitting, I could tell his build was stocky. He reminded me of a truck. Behind his eyes carried the look of horror and torment. He was smiling and laughing but it was a facade. I knew he was evil. There were no lights on; candles lit the room, faintly casting an eerie glow, and their flickering caused shadows to dance around the walls.

The pounding rain and winds outside were muffled as I could barely hear their savage howls. I walked towards the windows and noticed they were covered from the outside. The baby's room window had not been covered? I had been able to look out and see the storm beyond the window.

Perplexed, I followed the hallway back to the baby's room. The windows were now boarded from the outside. For a brief second, I remembered I was in a dream and anything is possible. Just then a clap of thunder and lightning crashed through the sky. The sound bounced through my head and I jumped right out of my dream.

Jerry was still pleasantly sleeping beside me, unaware of the monsoon living and breathing outside. I snuggled in closer and once again tried to go back to sleep. My mind was unable to rest and kept flowing back to the evil revolting man. His face was now etched in my mind. He had been the man in my other dream; the one who had chased me.

Dr. Reisen

I dragged myself into work not at all my normal *ray of sunshine*. I didn't even know what day of the week it was. I hadn't slept except for the freakish dream which left my internal organs in a knot tighter than a constrictor. Jerry didn't believe me, and I had an appointment with a doctor in psychic shit. Was that even possible? I had decided Dr. Reisen was my best chance at getting my life back.

For lunch, Jerry took me to Hoagie World. It was my favorite sandwich shop but the wrenching in my gut took away my appetite. With listless determination, I managed a few bites of my chicken Caesar.

"Are you upset over our conversation last night?" he asked.

"No... actually, yes. You need to believe me. I saw the woman and it stormed just as I predicted." No matter how preposterous it sounded, I had something to say. "After you went to sleep last night, she came back. She was outside my bedroom window. I went outside to check it out."

"You went outside?" he interrupted.

"Yes, she was gone, of course, but two small female shoeprints were left behind. I'm sure they're gone now because the rain washed them away but I saw them. I came inside and went to sleep and had that recurring dream again." I went on to explain the dream in detail.

"Maybe I was too quick to look for simple logic. It could be that you have a stalker," he said with a hint of sarcasm.

"Well, I have an appointment today with a Dr. Reisen in Hatters Park."

"What type of doctor is he?" Jerry inquired.

"She," I stressed, "Is a doctor who works with and studies the paranormal."

"You can't be serious?"

"I am. The appointment is at a quarter after four and Joe has agreed to let me leave early." That was it. I was going. *Why couldn't he just take a leap of faith? Was it so strange?* Yes, it was. The entire situation was chaotic!

"I'm coming with you," he stated.

"You don't believe me! No, you stay here. I'll call you when I get in touch with the dead." The rest of the meal was quiet.

The traffic to Hatters Park wasn't as obscene as I thought it would be and I reached her office by ten after four. My phone buzzed softly in my pocket, assuming it was Jerry, I willfully ignored it.

Her office wasn't what I expected. There were no crystal balls or tarot decks and it was painted a pastel blue with creamy yellow curtains. Her secretary was a gentleman about my age. He had a long face with a hawk-like nose and thin hair that was smoothed back into a ponytail.

He moved with impeccable grace, "You must be Sunshine," carefully placing his hands over mine, he continued, "The first appointment is always free." Letting go of my hands and grasping his together in front of his chest he said, "Dr. Reisen is expecting you."

He guided me to her office. He was so graceful that he appeared to float. The door glided open with his gentle push. OK, maybe I was a little creeped out. "Your four fifteen is here." His voice was even poetic.

"Thank you," came a voice stemming from behind a gigantic velvet chair. He floated out of her office.

Dr. Reisen swiveled her chair around. I fully expected her to have a huge wart dangling on the edge of her horned nose, instead she was pleasant looking.

Actually, she was a very attractive woman who couldn't have been a day over forty. Her hair was blond and styled short. She wore a dark purple polyester jacket, accentuating the whiteness of her skin, which came down tight around her chest and frilled at the waist. The collar of her jacket stood at attention around her neck as if starched in a vertical position. Her skirt was white and came down to her ankles with purple flowers sprinkling the fabric. On her feet she had open toed gold sandals with a three inch heel. Stones flared brilliantly, carried inside gold and silver bands around each of her fingers. Around her neck was a thick gold chain with a purple flower that fell just beneath her breasts. Matching ear rings dangled loosely beneath her impeccably styled blond plumage. She looked a little like Dracula's wife and I half expected wings to form off her back and sharp canines to dig into my neck, leaving me bloodless.

Dr. Reisen motioned me to sit on a chaise that looked more like a shrink's couch. "Sunshine please, tell me why you are here?"

I was feeling a little intimidated and clumsy at the moment. "I'm not sure where to start," I said settling my butt onto the chaise. "I think I may have a twin who's trying to tell me something. I thought I had figured it out but she's still haunting me."

"Haunting you? Is she dead?" she queried.

"No, she's very much alive but I never knew she existed until a few weeks ago when she turned up in the hospital."

She tapped her long acrylic French manicured fingernails together, "She is sick?"

"Yeah, kind of. She had a really bad accident."

"What is it you want me to help you with?" She asked.

"Can people with head trauma start experiencing psychic episodes or gain psychic abilities?"

"Oh yes. It happens quite frequently. Now, is it her that has the head trauma? Is that why she is in the hospital?"

"Yes, I have been experiencing her thoughts and memories for a few weeks now and I knew we looked similar. I went to the hospital the other day to see for myself. We share the same birthday and look identical except our hair color. She has… mahogany colored hair." An epiphany unloaded on my brain at that exact moment. "Like the father in my dream." I blurted out.

She leaned forward and asked, "You are having dreams about her, too?"

"No, she's never in them. It's like a recurring dream but every time I have it, I see more."

She replied, "Tell me more about your dreams." I went on and explained each one with fantastic detail. She sat back in her huge purple chair that threatened to swallow her whole. An entire foot of the chair must have extended above her head.

"Tell me more about this woman you believe is your twin?" She seemed genuinely interested and I spilled my guts, everything except the part about me and Jay.

She nodded her head and asked, "I'm not sure what is happening to you is psychic. You may be having repressed memories. The episode you experienced in Chesterville may be a memory related to her, but this person you are seeing and the woman in your dreams may be something else entirely. Would you be willing to undergo hypnosis?"

Jerry would call off the wedding if I told him I was considering it. At this point, I figured what was there to lose? I wanted this over and my life back in time for my wedding.

She must have read my wavering mind because she spoke again. "I don't practice hypnosis myself. A good friend and long-time colleague of mine does. He has a valid list of credentials and PHD's including physcogenics, spiritual psychology, and hypnotherapy. He is one of the best, and we have combined our skills on many occasions to assist people in their beyond the physical realm dilemmas. You don't have to give me an answer now."

She stood up and walked to her desk, opening the top drawer, pulling out a small card. She then walked back and handed it to me. "Here is his card. Give him a call when you decide." I took the card, thanked her and left her office.

Outside, I took one last glance at the building fully expecting to see a pointy roof, three varied levels, and statuesque gargoyles peering down at me, but nope, it was the same building I had walked into an hour ago.

I had stuffed the card into my purse but now I took it out, his name is Dr. Weered. His office was located in Horn City. I plugged his name into a search engine and got his website and a couple articles. Scanning his website it said his specialty was hypnosis of repressed memories and dream interpretation. He believes past memories are connected to our subconscious and come forth in our dreams. I clicked back and chose an article. It appeared that he was highly recommended and maybe not a kook as his overly generic name would suggest. His work had been used in court cases and crime solving. The next day, I would call.

We Found It

The lively scent of the brewing coffee brought Jay to the front of my mind, slipping into a daydream which was abruptly interrupted as my phone started dancing across my desk. I had learned to keep it on vibrate since the bathtub incident. It was a text from Jerry *How did the appt go?*

Was he asking because he really wanted to know or because he wanted to be proven right? I texted back *She thinks it's not so much paranormal as it may be repressed memories.* What exactly are repressed memories anyways? *A memory that has been pressed once and then pressed again? Why not call them squelched or subdued memories?*

R U going back? Buzzed another message from Jerry. *Wouldn't he like to know?* The wisest course of action was probably not to mention the hypnosis I had at this very moment been contemplating.

I might was my response.

A small message box was blinking on my phone. Det. Henderson had called last night and left a voicemail, "The car turned up parked deep into the forest outside of Salvation Cove. They're towing it now. Crime guys will have it a couple days and the report won't be back for probably a week." A week, time was closing in on me. I needed this solved before then.

The scraggly dispatcher answered the phone, "Chesterville Sheriff, can I help ya?" The *ya* gave it away.

"Could I speak with Det. Henderson please?"

"Hold a second," said the voice. I imagined her in-desperate-need-of-a-fill acrylics punching his line.

A few seconds later, he answered, "Detective Henderson speaking."

"This is Sunshine. I just got your message. Any news yet?"

"Not much yet, the car looks clean, like whoever did it wiped down afterwards. Some fingerprints were taken off the wheel and I think a few strays of hair were found, most likely hers. Forensics has it now."

Patience is a virtue, I reminded myself.

"Thanks, give me a call when the report is in, please," I pleaded.

"Will do pretty lady."

Thursday afternoon at three thirty was my appointment with Dr. Weered. Until then I had decided to do some Eilida background research. If we were twins there would be a sparkle in our pasts, even if it was dim.

At the paper, I had a cornucopia of untapped resources. My time would not be spent idly waiting. I had her name and age but I didn't know much about her family or where she lived. I looked up the name Riley and a list of hundreds flooded my screen. I needed to narrow it down so I looked at the list of Rileys in the state. The list was still huge, but getting smaller. By the time I was done consolidating the list, only a few Rileys were left. I brought up courthouse documents for the few left. Hours later I found nothing, everyone was either too old or too young.

Tidbits from my dream surfaced *the windows were covered from the outside. They wanted to keep something out, the storm? What type of storm would be severe enough to cover your windows? A* hurricane, bingo! That left a wide area to cover. The entire southern half of the eastern seaboard experienced hurricanes. In order to narrow that down I decided to cross reference hurricanes with my birthday, wait no, the baby was about one and a half to two and a half years old. The work was tedious but with sheer determination I plugged away.

"You've been quiet today?" mentioned Joe as he strolled by my desk.

"I guess, I'm working on something, a hunch."

"The reporter is in you. It's addicting. Look around you, we thrive on it and now that you've discovered field work, you will, too."

Giggling, I responded, "I have the itch and it won't stop. I've gone so far as to give myself a deadline, June thirtieth, my wedding day."

"You let me know if this takes you out of town again. I think you have what it takes to make it." He was so supportive. I wished Jerry would be.

"Joe, do you believe in the paranormal, repressed memories, twins separated at birth?"

"Sure, some of it. Is that part of your research?"

I relayed to him my thoughts, only I left me and Eilida out of it. I gave him a seed, hoping for a carrot. "I like it. You get the goods on that and we'll run it front page."

My heart skipped a beat, "Really?"

"You research it, keep me informed and you write it."

"Thursday, I'm visiting a hypnotist as part of this. I'll need to leave about three in the afternoon."

"You got it and one more thing," he said, handing me an envelope. "Your check for expenses in Chesterville." I hadn't expected any reimbursement. I could play around; dig into people's lives at someone else's expense, wow! I would have to send him my bill from Dr. Weered.

Dr. Wolfgang Weered

The office of Dr. Weered will remain unforgettable in my mind. He had two deer heads with enormous antlers hanging high on his walls not far below his ten foot ceilings. Instead of a secretary he had a nurse. Her uniform looked like a Halloween costume. A traditional nurse's hat sat upon her heavily sprayed hair which poofed beneath the hat and then fell long and straight, pooling at the bottom. What little skirt she had edged very close to her fanny and buxom double D's flopped out of a rigid cotton top.

She greeted me with a high pitched squeal, "Welcome to Doctor Weered's office. If you'll take a seat in one of the chairs," motioning to a row of semi comfy looking chairs, "And fill this out, we'll be right with you." She handed me a clip board and I took a seat.

The questions were typical doctor office questions, any allergies, illness, medications. The list went on and on for three pages, front and back. It might be easier to give a blood sample. The last page was a disclaimer. To sum it up it stated if anything happened here he would not be held accountable. *What might happen?* Would I leave his office disoriented or squawking like a chicken every time I heard a bell? I signed anyways and handed Ms. Halloween back the clipboard.

"Do you have insurance?" I was unaware that insurance covered hypnosis. I opened my wallet and gave her my card. She walked to the copy machine, her skirt becoming dangerously close to baring her bootie. "That will be sixty dollars, cash or charge?" I gave her my bank card which she returned a few seconds later with my insurance card and a receipt for me to sign.

Within a couple minutes, a man dressed in scrubs strolled through a doorway and called me back. He took my height, weight, and blood pressure. "Everything's good. If you'll wait in here, the doctor will be right with you." Using his right hand, he pushed open a door.

As soon as I entered the room, the door swung shut and I was alone. The room had macabre written all over it. Another deer head stared down at me through lifeless eyes. Outstretched arms with curled claws lurked at me from a grizzly bear perched in the corner. A snarl buckled his nose with gnarled teeth jutting out from his jaw. Panic rushed through me and I floundered backwards for a fraction of a second as I thought he was real and I was dinner. His cousin lay on the floor as a rug between two guest chairs which faced a desk and a darker than night leather couch. I assumed the couch was for his patients. The room itself had an eerie glow about it.

I was officially freaked out and ready to run when the door burst open and a presumably Dr. Weered walked in. Thick hair covered his head and came to a V shaped point on his forehead. A full chunky beard wrapped around his face barely exposing two eyes and a nose. He was a stout man and no more than a few inches taller than me. Furry hair covered his arms and stuck out from his rolled up dress shirt sleeves, sweat puddled around his armpits. I fully expected him to transform into a werewolf before my eyes, his body contorting and writhing throughout the process.

A congenial voice sliced through the air and eased my tension, "I'm Dr. Weered and you must be Sunshine," he said flipping through my three pages of paperwork. That is how the session started.

After several minutes of talking about my reason for being there and him explaining what hypnosis really is and what I could expect, his medical assistant, the man who took my blood pressure, strolled in. He explained that Jonathon was always present during sessions and insisted I lay on the couch. In the background, soft music played and he spoke in a soothing voice. Soon, I was swept away but I could still hear him.

"Think of a time when you were most happy." My mind flowed back in time to my sixteenth birthday.

"My sixteenth birthday," I replied.

"Use your senses, what do you see, what do you hear?"

"I see my room, it's a Saturday and the delicious smells of homemade sausage and gravy drifted upstairs to my room. I followed the scent and mom was in the kitchen, her chest to the oven. Dad was setting the table. 'Happy birthday honey,' he said giving me a hug. Mom set the food on the table and joined in the hug. We finished breakfast and they handed me a card. Anxiously, I opened the card and a key on a rhinestone decorated chain fell out.

""A car, my own car!" I shouted running out the door. A beautiful maroon coupé sat in the driveway. I quickly unlocked the door and jumped in. My parents stood in the doorway, all smiles.

""Get in, we're going for a drive," I screeched with joy. My mom went back inside and grabbed her purse, soon she was back and we left. I drove to Sage's and honked the horn. Peering at me from her window she laughed and disappeared. The garage door opened and she came running out. We jumped up and down for a few minutes and she climbed in."

"On the count of three you will return to my office, one… two… three."

I was no longer in my memory but in his office. "Do you remember what you experienced?"

"I do and…" I had trouble finding the words because I was utterly confused. "It wasn't my memory. The car, it's like mine but the wrong color and I didn't get it for my sixteenth birthday. My parents - they're not mine they are Jerry's and the house is theirs too and Sage isn't my friend. These are Eilida's memories confused with my own."

Through the hair that covered his face, I could see the sincerity in his eyes, "Hypnosis isn't a perfect science and it affects everyone differently. It is not uncommon to have confused or untrue recollections of events. I would like you to come back for another session sometime early next week," he said in his soothing voice. A part of my subconscious yearned to know these memories. I made an appointment with Ms. Halloween and headed home.

It was nearly five and a message from Jerry asked me to meet him for dinner at six. That didn't give me much time. Rush hour traffic had the freeway backed up, so I swung off at the next exit and took the back roads. GPS was awesome.

Eilida

Sage came home with me and we spent the day decorating the house and calling friends. Late in the afternoon we hopped in my racy little car, went to the video store, and got the zombie movie trilogy *The Lost Dead, The Undead,* and *Dead, Dead, Dead.* Priscilla and Kaila joined us that night and we ordered our favorite pizza, Italian sausage and pineapple.

After my parents went to bed, we snuck into the house bar - it was always fully stocked - and stole a few beers. With our beer, we followed the dirt path to the lake and dangled our feet in the water.

"It's freezing," shouted Kaila as she yanked her foot out.

"Quiet, I hear something," Sage whispered. She fanned her hands out to motion our silence. "There it is again," she stated in a barely audible whisper and gave me a wink.

"Blaaah," I shouted and pushed Sage into the water. A few seconds later her head popped up and Priscilla, Kaila and I crumpled over in laughter. The look on Sage's face was priceless as she pulled herself onto the dock and rolled in laughter with us.

She guffawed, "That water is friggin' cold."

Hurricane Chloe

Sunshine

My GPS took me directly to the restaurant where Jerry was already waiting. Greeting me with tender loving arms, he asked, "How was your day?" That would be a rhetorical question but he had no idea where I'd been so I took it as conversation. My story had worked so well with Joe that I thought I would try one on Jerry.

"I've been researching hurricanes. Since I broke open the case in Chesterville, Joe thinks I should take on something else." That seemed reasonable.

"Hurricanes - you remember my friend Hank? He is a meteorologist and specializes in tropical disturbances. I bet he could give you some useful information."

"Thank you! I've been trying to find hurricanes from twenty to twenty two years ago. I need to find survivors. Uh, Det. Henderson called me today. They found Eilida's car. The forensics team isn't done with it yet but he'll call me back when they are. He doesn't know anything, yet."

"Impressive, you already have connections and you've been a part time reporter for only two weeks," he said, his eyebrows lifted and mouth punched out in approval. He then asked, "Have you talked to my mom lately?"

"No. I need to call her so we can work out the details for my bridal shower."

"On the phone today she said something about booking a limousine." His attempt to distract me, and a good one it was. I allowed it and went with the flow. In a couple short weeks, I would be his wife.

The following day, I called Jerry's friend Hank and he agreed to meet with me at one thirty in the afternoon at the bagel shop across the street. The time was now ten after one. I informed Joe I would be across the street and slung my purse over my shoulder and was out the door. By twenty after one, I was grabbing the handle on the door to the bagel shop. Someone caught the door behind me and finished opening it. I turned back to thank him and realized it was Hank. We exchanged greetings and he ordered us a couple coffees which we took to a booth by the window.

"I found a list of hurricanes in the time range you were interested in. I cross referenced them with survivors and it's a long list. The most memorable hurricane of that time was Chloe. She was a sleeper, everyone knew she was out there but she was barely a category two with wind speeds hovering around ninety six, ninety seven miles per hour, until just before landfall when she gained strength and hit the shore with a hundred twenty eight mile winds and gusts much higher, a near CAT 4. Once inland she fizzled out quickly but the area was devastated and a few families local to the area didn't bother to evacuate."

My head was spinning, "Where?"

"In Billows Hollow on June 30th, 1992."

Stunned, I asked, "Could you repeat the date?" He knew it by heart and repeated, "June 30th 1992."

"My wedding date is on the twenty first anniversary of Hurricane Chloe?" It wasn't really a question but more of a bombshell.

"It is, don't be too hard on yourself. You didn't know."

The date echoed in my head. He handed me a stack of print outs and said, "It's been nice seeing you and I'll be expecting that invitation," He held my hand, lifting it to his lips and planted a small kiss.

I smiled and returned with, "Mailing them out this week."

What he gave me about Hurricane Chloe was more analytical than compassionate. *Chloe, Chloe, Chloe,* it was more than a name, rather something that I had known subliminally.

Survivors of Hurricane Chloe, one letter at a time, traced across my computer screen. Immediately, a list of articles from local papers and video clips from TV stations rolled up and down my screen. I spent the rest of the afternoon reading and watching. Time was running out and five o'clock was a mere fifteen minutes away. I printed out the last couple remaining stories.

Thunder and lightning tore through the angry sky with cumbersome clouds that jeopardized my ride home. I had barely made it through the door when an effusion of water blasted hard against the sidewalk splashing against the backs of my legs as the door swung shut. Now it was on the outside and I was safe.

Safety these days has become relative, I thought as I ambled up the stairs and maybe it was the hurricane project I had become so absorbed in but I didn't like the rain, the clouds, thunder, and lightning. It all made me edgy.

Jerry strolled through my door at approximately six p.m., punctual as usual. He leaned his umbrella against the hall outside my door. The bottom of his pant legs and shoes drenched from the rain. One at a time he slipped off his shoes and left them in the entryway then sauntered my way and wrapped his arms around my waist. "How's my Sunshine?"

"Wonderful now that you're here," I divulged returning his hug, my lips saluted in return to his affection.

"Were you able to talk to Hank?"

"Oh yes, he met me today at the bagel shop." I declared with no follow up.

After a few seconds, he nudged, "And?"

I turned to the fridge and busied myself with unloading our makings for dinner, with my back to him I responded, "He gave me a lot of information on tropical weather, and pointed out a specific hurricane that snuck up on a small town, Billows Hollow, nearly twenty one years ago." I left out the piece about our wedding falling on its anniversary.

"Good. Anything you can use for your story?"

"Maybe, I did some additional research and may have found something," a hero story stuck in my mind but I hadn't yet read the entire piece. "An officer, I think her name was Burkhalder, seemed to be active in the recovery process. I want to interview her."

"Is she still in Billows Hollow?" he questioned.

"I don't know but I'll find out tomorrow when I call, if I can get hold of her. I may have to leave town again."

"Billows Hollow, my parents have a summer home on the beach there. I'm sure you can stay in it if you need to. It's a little ways outside of town but…"

I cut him off, "Thanks, I'll keep that in mind."

After dinner, we finished our wedding invitations, leaving my mouth with a lingering nasty gluey taste from licking so many envelopes. Tendrils of water continued to seep down my window even though the storm had subsided.

Session Two

Officer Burkhalder no longer worked directly for the Sheriff's office, she was now more of a consultant and part time private investigator. I left my work and cell number with another officer and waited for her return call.

The day proved busy with menial tasks, answering the phone, taking messages, and patching calls through. On the outskirts of town a transformer blew and with it several homes had lost electricity. That was big news in Lyden today but within a few hours the power company had everyone's homes up and running again.

My second appointment with Dr. Weered, the wolf man with the tender voice, the gentle giant, was the next evening. When I arrived, immediately I was escorted to his office by Jonathon, Dr. Reisen was present as well. I hadn't expected that. In contrast, they looked like a werewolf with his vampire bride. *Did vampires and werewolves even like each other?* A question I didn't really want to know, especially at my expense.

Dr. Reisen didn't interfere, her high collar starched upwards against her neck, just watched. The soothing music washed away my tenseness and his tender voice put me into what he called a hyperattentive state, meaning, according to Weered, that I was focused on his voice allowing my subconscious mind to take over.

"Tell me about your earliest memory," said my voice guide.

In the voice of a very young child I elaborated. "I'm four and I can't sleep from the rain outside. It keeps beating on my window and I think the beast is going to get me. He has no hair and eyes like black marbles."

"Relax, is anybody with you?" asks Dr. Weered in his lulling voice

"No, I'm in my bed but I run to my parents' room and curl up in bed next to them. Daddy wakes up and whispers, 'Eilida what's wrong?'

"'Can't sleep daddy, the beast man is outside my window.' Daddy props his head in his hand and says, 'Nobody's there, it's the rain, do you want me to check?'

"'No!' I holler. My mommy wakes up then and curls me to her, 'Go to sleep baby, go to sleep'."

"Let's jump ahead, tell me about Sunshine?"

"She works at the paper with me as our receptionist. I call her Sunshine because she is always perky no matter how horrible the day is. She smiles twenty four seven. She has lived in Chesterville most of her life I think, maybe. Anyways, I know she was head cheer leader, homecoming queen, prom queen, and took ballet and gymnastics until she was fifteen, sixteen. She's told me all about it. Most of the time her peppiness is too much, but occasionally we talk."

"Tell me about Eilida?" Prompted Dr. Weered.

"I have a column, Dear Delilah, and work mostly out of my home. The article doesn't take any crazy literary talent, but one day I hope to be a journalist. I'm twenty three and nearly done with my associates degree. My next step is to attend the University with a major in journalism. I have sent my application and am waiting for their response."

"On the count of three, you will return, one... two... three..."

Eilida

Since remembering Sage, I hadn't been able to stop thinking about her. I would be finishing my college career full time at the University and we had never been separated since the day we switched snacks in Kindergarten. She was far more than my best friend. I hadn't told her, couldn't tell her, until my acceptance was official. My heart wanted her to go with me for its own selfish reasons. She had her own dreams to follow through with. I didn't want us to part ways and lose track of one another.

When I moved in to Grandma's she jumped at the opportunity, we both did, it was freedom from our parents and we lingered in community college for as long as we could. She is the only person in my life who has always been there and listened to my paranoid suspicions. I have told her all the chilling details about my nightmares where I'm being chased by the bald man with his beady eyes. I'm outside in the rain and he materializes out of the grey surrounding me and I run until a wooden trunk coalesces from the ground, but I can't reach the chest. I feel its pull but I always wake up before I can open the lid. Sometimes he carries a dagger coated in blood that drips from its jagged point.

My memories have been pouring into my mind at an exponential rate. It's like my subconscious has been dormant and now has awoken. The beast from within aches to free itself from the chains that tie me. The chains that keep me posted to this bed where my family and friends take vigilant watch over me.

Sunshine

The fur around Dr. Weered's mouth moved softly up and down as he spoke, "We are making good progress, Sunshine. You have begun to recollect so much."

"But they aren't my memories?"

He smiled and the hair around his mouth rose up, moving into his nose, "But, I think they are. The clarity of them and how you never falter reassures they are yours."

"I'm not Eilida, my name is Sunshine."

"And so it is. Your next session I would like to go back to your childhood. That is where we will find the answers." I wasn't sure I wanted another session, nor was I sure why I remembered her life so clearly and not my own.

Up to this point, Dr. Reisen sat quietly without muttering so much as a word. "Sunshine, this is not my area of expertise but I watched and listened to you. Dr. Weered and I have worked closely through many years and I have sat in on many hypnotherapy sessions and I find yours rare and genuine. You think this young lady is your twin and there is a very real probability she is."

Behind her eyes, I could see her searching for the correct words to pull out. "It would be my strong recommendation for you to continue. Your mind believes you are Eilida and the only way to break through that barrier is to keep going."

Her words jarred my psyche, the sessions were genuine, *was I Eilida?* I couldn't be, she's in a hospital bed and I'm here. The connection we share is strong, no doubt. As I pondered my dilemma I allowed the door to swing shut behind me and through the silence of the air I overheard, "Her mind is convinced… It is possible for identical twins to communicate telepathically without realizing it… These recollections are hers." Now I was a case study for two scientists to debate over.

Denial

An hour into work, a fiftyish woman walked through the door. Her slacks swished as she walked and looked out of place next to her running shoes. Her blouse was buttoned loosely around the waist displaying a tank top underneath. Shoulder length dark auburn hair framed her tough facial exterior and helped to soften it.

"Lyden Times, can I assist you?" I asked as when she arrived at my desk.

"Are you Sunshine?" *She knew me?*

"I am and you are?"

"The former Detective Burkhalder."

"Oh, please forgive me. You really didn't have to drive all the way here, I would have happily driven to Billows Hollow."

Her tough expression was going nowhere, it was plastered on like a bad paint job. She continued, "Can we talk privately?"

"Allow me fifteen minutes and I'll meet you across the street," I suggested.

"I'll be at the coffee shop." Her stern eyes made me feel as though I was a child in deep doodoo.

She was waiting at the coffee shop as promised. Glances of a young headstrong Burkhalder in a black police woman's uniform flashed through my mind as I took a seat across from her. "Detective Burkhalder, I will get to the point. I have been researching Hurricane Chloe. Your name continues to pop up during my research. You were there and I would like some personal insight into the story. Details about the storm and any rescue stories you may be willing to share."

"That was a long time ago," she said. Her voice was as hard as her face.

"I understand if it's too difficult. That was your community and your home. The piece I'm doing is a reflection of the good in the community, not the devastation."

"I was much younger, hadn't been a Detective for more than a year and I was wet around the collar. It's a small community. The worst we deal with is local drunks and tourists. That storm really took us by surprise," her eyes became soulful as she continued the story. "The beach front was in shambles, pieces of homes rolled in and out with the tide. Luckily, most of them were vacation homes, others evacuated at the last minute causing a helluva traffic jam. Only a few families remained."

I listened intently as she progressed. "Surprisingly, there were only four deaths but they were my friends, Jim Tate and his family.

I had known him most of my life. He had a beautiful wife, Lilly. She had the blackest hair I've ever seen. They were a handsome couple and their children." She paused for a moment.

"If this is too difficult, we don't have to continue."

Her lips curled into a slight smile and she went on. "It's been nearly twenty one years. Where was I? Oh yeah. They had the most adorable children and their little girl, she was rescued. Somehow the storm had spared her life, such a little thing. Her brown ringlets stuck to her face and she cried. A stranger found her and picked her up from the rubbage. I held her in my arms and brought her to the medics. It was amazing she hadn't a scratch on her and was in perfect health, with the exception of undernourishment, but a few good meals took care of that. Her aunt and uncle collected her and I haven't seen her since."

"That's a beautiful story. Do you remember the young girl's name?"

"I'll never be able to forget it, Eilida, Eilida Tate."

Goosebumps shot across my body and my heartbeat quickened. *Is Eilida Riley Eilida Tate?*

She placed her elbows on the table and leaned her torso forward in my direction. "Sweetie, I've spent many years as a police officer and I've worked with a lot of reporters and you, darling, are no reporter, so why the interest in Hurricane Chloe?"

A cold sweat beaded up on my forehead. How did I think I could fool a hard-nosed detective like her? Should I spill my guts? She had given me a cornucopia of information. I wasn't yet sure how it tied me and Eilida together or even if it did, but my twin, parapsychology, repressed memory theory wasn't something I was going to elaborate on with her. In the end, I decided to play it cool and naive.

"You're right. I'm what you would call 'Wet around the collar.' Several weeks ago, a young woman suffered a tragic accident and my heart went out to her. The entire community of Lyden went out to her, pulling resources together and eventually assisting in identifying her. As a chance of fate, I ended up being the person who went to her home town, and working with a detective there we broke the case open, the cause for her tragedy anyways. The experience sparked my interest in the business and now I'm trying to learn more about her. Her name is Eilida Riley. Do you think she is Eilida Tate?"

The intimidation move was over and she rested her back against the booth again. "They are the same person. Her aunt and uncle's name was Riley and they legally adopted her shortly after taking her in. I said I haven't seen her since, I didn't say I haven't kept up with her. She was only two years old, my place as her father's friend had ended. I didn't want to continue in her life; a constant memory of that horrible night."

I offered, "She is still at the hospital here if you would like to glance in."

"She is the reason I'm here, unfinished business. It was nice to meet you Sunshine, but our talk is over." She pulled her approximately five foot six 150 pound frame out from the booth and was gone.

Detective Burkhalder was clever and lacking in the social skills department. She withheld the entire story, I knew that. I got the details she deemed were important for me to know and only a little more than I already knew. The story about the girl was front page news but her name was withheld. She gave me a bone and now I had to chew on it, *unfinished business, what unfinished buisness?* Am I the unfinished piece? I had names, Jim and Lilly Tate. After several minutes of contemplating Burkhalder's story and my hypno-sessions, thoughts swirled to a central point within my head. My ghost wasn't Eilida at all but someone she resembles. I still lacked any theory on how I tied into any of this. A buzzing came from inside my purse, pulling out my phone I saw Detective Henderson had called.

Eilida

In an effort to keep my memory train going, my dad brought over some homemade videos. The first was on my tenth birthday. I was running around, playing with Sage and some other friends and stuffing my face with a barbecued burger and chocolate cake. I didn't look like I had a care in the world. Our house was huge and beautiful, surrounded by vividly colored trees and flowers. Large white columns, plantation style, supported an awning that covered the wraparound porch and a horseshoe drive curved around the front.

Inside, we had a spiral staircase, more times than I can count I rode down the wooden banister and got scolded for it. What child could resist the temptation of sliding down such a staircase, accelerating until they fell upon pillows placed strategically on the floor? I was never alone; my partner in crime was always by my side, my surrogate sister, Sage.

Outside the door, a redheaded brunette was talking to my parents. The conversation became heated. In her agitated state, I heard my mother say, "No, no she doesn't."

The brunette woman sternly looked into her eyes and said, "She knows, she will be able to identify him." Lip reading wasn't an exact science but I'm ninety nine percent sure that's what she said. Me, were they talking about me? *Who would I be able to identify?*

The brunette pointed towards my door, "Why do you think he's here?"

My father spoke up then, "Absolutely not, it would destroy her. We have had her since she was two, she's our daughter. Maybe when she's fully recovered, we will revisit. Now you will have to excuse us, we have videos to watch with our daughter." My father placed his arm around my mother's waist; they turned their backs to her and strolled back into my room.

"Denial," mouthed the brunette from under her breath.

Sunshine

As soon as the opportunity presented I returned Det. Henderson's call.

"Forensics found something. One of the hairs they plucked out of the car turned out to be someone other than Eilida's."

"Whose?" I asked.

"I'd rather tell you in person. I can be there Monday afternoon." I looked at the time, it was four thirty eight; Monday would have to do.

"Give me a call when you get to town, thanks."

"You got it, pretty lady."

One Dimensional

I had to get home, my soon to be mother and father in law would be here within a couple hours for our bachelor/ bachelorette parties tomorrow, and dinner was at Outlandies seven o'clock sharp. Outlandies was a swank establishment which required I dressed my best. With the exception of work, my attire as of late consisted of shorts, tanks, and flip flops.

The warm water from the shower head sprayed as it caressed my back and torso. It felt great and I allowed a few extra minutes of shower time. I lingered long enough in the shower to fog up the mirror. I took my hand towel and wiped the moisture off the mirror, leaning in close I applied my makeup waiting for my ghost. She didn't appear and never appeared when I wanted her to. I had questions for her if I wasn't too scared upon her next visit to ask.

I styled my hair into soft curls that fell across my chest and back. Carefully, I lifted a red shift above my head and let it drop around my shoulders. It had an asymmetrical hem which flowed behind me as I walked and flared when I spun. I wrapped a gold scarf around my waist and topped off the guise with a pair of red prism heals that sparkled as the light bounced off the tiny embedded rhinestones. A picture is worth a thousand words I thought as I blinked at myself in the mirror.

We went out to eat two to three nights a week but not to places as ritzy as Outlandies. The building was painted lilac on the outside. Inside were square tables angled so they appeared as diamonds. Glass bowls with floating candles were arranged in the middles over violet-sapphire table cloths. The walls were painted a bluish-grey and made to look antique and weather worn with cracks and uneven splotches throughout. Large fake plants were set sparingly in corners and viney greenery sprawled along the ledges.

Jerry and I were escorted to a corner table which allowed for privacy. He ordered a bottle of cabernet sauvignon while we waited. I had never understood why wines had to have such strange names.

"Why don't you tell me about the latest in your case?" Jerry inquired. Within the secrecy of my own head, I thought *where do I start and how much had I already told him?*

"Did I tell you they found some evidence in her car?"

Puzzled, he asked, "Whose car?"

"I haven't told you? Eilida's car."

He scrunched his eyebrows downward into thin slits and asked, "I thought you had wrapped that up and it was over?"

Had I given him that impression or is that what he wanted? "It is over, but Detective Henderson promised to keep me up on the details surrounding the incident."

He resigned the battle and released his expression with a sigh, "Hhh… What did they find?"

"I don't know yet, he's coming by Monday and will let me know then. Enough about me," I wanted to end this quickly before I spewed out the story Detective Burkhalder had given me today, "How was your day?"

"I punch numbers and guide my client's finances." His sarcasm pushed a dagger through me. Suddenly, he stood and said, "Mom, Dad," and then he gave them each a hug. I had been saved and the tension eased.

I hadn't noticed until that night how similar in appearance his and Eilida's parents appeared, had I? *Hypnosis isn't a perfect science and it affects everyone differently. It is not uncommon to have confused or untrue recollections of events,* Dr. Weered's words. I resolved to believe that I was mixing his parents into my confused memories, which didn't belong to me anyways, but Eilida. Throughout dinner, we discussed the festivities of the weekend.

The plan had been for all of us to spend the weekend at Jerry's. My sixth sense warned against it, however it may continue to ease the tension if I did. My bag was already packed and in his trunk.

Jerry's house was a simple ranch style three bedroom two bath house. His parents had one of the extra rooms and I got the other. Up to this very moment, I had never considered why we so seldom spent time here. His place was neat, orderly and sparsely accessorized with modern style furnishings. Soon, I would be living here with him. I examined the place with my wifey eyes. The house was cold and impersonal, devoid of anything that might say, "I'm Jerry and this is my humble home". His walls were near bare with the exception of his forty inch plasma hanging from the living room wall. It is commonly known that your home is a reflection of who you are. At this juncture, I asked myself *who is Jerry?* A one dimensional man. *Is this the man I am getting ready to marry?* I will have to add some color and life into this dismal but orderly home.

The bedroom I stayed in had a twin bed with starched flat sheets that felt cold and inflexible against my back. Unable to sleep, I moseyed into the kitchen for a drink. Everyone else was asleep and an ambiguous silence fell through the air and surrounded me. I felt like I was in a dream lurking around a haunted home. With every step I expected a poltergeist to sail down from the ceiling and take charge of my body or find a zombie hunkered in a corner eating Jerry's flesh.

In the kitchen I rummaged through his refrigerator, listening behind my back the entire time. The contents inside were catalogued into groups, and unopened like he never ate. His cabinets were the same, all labels facing out and nothing out of place, *creepy*. A breeze against my back told me I wasn't alone. I turned slowly and my ghost sat at the table, her head down and dark hair flowing long and twisted.

I'm not scared; I'm not scared I chanted to myself as I moved towards her. *I'm not scared, I'm not scared*, and she was now in front of me. Anxiety cropped up within the pit of my stomach and crested. I took a deep breath and slowly, gingerly raised my hand to touch her. If she was a ghost, my hand would go through. If she was something more then I probably wouldn't live to know what. Ever so close, my hand continued its journey towards her. My fingers dangled beside her bent-in shoulders. "Mrs…" I started to say.

But my words were interrupted from behind when I heard a female voice say, "Couldn't sleep either?"

I turned abruptly to see Jerry's mom standing in the entrance way. By the time I swung my head back, my ghost was gone.

The entire day I kept looking to the table hoping to see her there. She gave me both a panicky and serene feeling all at one time. As close as I had been able to get, I knew she wasn't Eilida but someone or something else. My suspicions of who still unconfirmed. I only knew she was someone who wandered this planet with a story to display to me when the timing was right.

Bachelorette Party

The limousine arrived on time at eight o'clock. It was white, inside colorful lights glowed from the headliner. The seating was arranged parallel the long ways and small liquor bottles and soda filled a mini fridge. Soft music played above us but I was unable to locate the speakers. The music came from all around like in my dream. The driver was young, tall, with wispy straight hair falling from his shoulders. I had seen him before yet for the life of me I was unable to place from where or when.

Our first stop was at the hotel to pick up my bridesmaids Priscilla and Kaila. After came our first club. We had decided on a night clubbing while Jerry and his friends had gone the traditional male route which I'm sure consisted of strippers and titty bars. I couldn't see any of that being Jerry's forte but it was his party and his best man had planned the entire event for him. Excitement unleashed fluttered around inside me and I was more than ready for my night of forbidden fun to begin.

It was in the first club that I noticed a short bald man looking my way. His shifty small black eyes pierced my soul from across the packed room. A few quick drinks later and I was having too good a time to pay him much attention.

"Ready for our next stop?" asked Kaila as she danced her way over to me, her radiant energy beaming in all directions. We had spent all of thirty minutes there and I was feeling the buzz.

"Let's go!"

A few clubs later, I had all but forgotten the creepy man and I was more than feeling good, actually I was completely inebriated and stumbling all over the place. I found I couldn't take a step forward without leaning harshly to either my right or left. Priscilla, Kaila and I were in a circle bumping butts, staggering, and making fools of ourselves when a flashback of my first evening with Jay came to the edge of my mind and rested. I suddenly went flying forward into Kaila with a hard butt push from behind. Kaila stumbled backwards from the force. We barely managed to hold each other up.

"Watch out!" hollered Priscilla.

"I'm so sorry," said a familiar voice that made every hair on my body salute. By the time our footing was reestablished and I was able to turn myself around all I saw was light glinting off a bald head as the body it belonged to ambled through the thickly packed club. Icicles crawled up my body starting at my feet not resting until they got to my head.

"Rude was that," said Kaila instead of *that was rude.* Her intoxicated tongue was unable to put the words in the correct order.

"Just some older guy, this place is too crowded. I know a place that's not. You ready to blow this joint?" responded Priscilla.

"I'm ready," I agreed.

The next club was less densely packed and we had more room on the floor where we hopefully wouldn't get bumped into. It was dark and more of a seedy bar than a club. Blue lights twinkled above our heads and a band played from the stage. No more than a handful of people drunkenly swayed across the dance floor. We sat at a booth located near an outside window.

Kaila's mouth drew up higher on one side displaying disgust, "That man over there keeps staring at us. It's creeping me out."

"What man?" asked Priscilla and I in sync with each other.

"The bald one at the end of the bar," she answered. Priscilla and I had to twist our heads backwards in order to see.

"Don't do that, he'll notice."

"Since we don't have eyes in the back of our heads how else are we going to see him?" I asked.

"I don't know; maybe get up and use the restroom, order another drink or something."

Priscilla and I arose from our seats and walked quietly to the dance floor. We casually started spinning and turning to the beat in order to get a look at him. After a few minutes, about the time I realized how dizzy the twirling had made me, we were both able to catch sight of him. "I think I've seen him tonight. He's so ugly that I haven't forgotten that face." I jested.

Turning again, Priscilla got a good look at him, "He was the man from the last club. The one who bumped into you, disturbing, he's stalking us." suggested Priscilla with a quivering edge to her voice.

No sooner had we got back to our seats and Kaila leaned in asking, "Did you see him?"

"Yeah, we did," said Priscilla and I in unison.

Priscilla offered, "He's the man who bumped into Sunshine at the last place. I think he's stalking us."

Jerry's mom jumped in then, "Maybe we should call it a night." The motherly voice of reason, translation - I'm tired, let's go.

I didn't feel so drunk anymore and spoke my words of reason. "No, if he's following us then he will follow us home. I saw him at the first bar and I agree with Priscilla he's stalking us. I don't want him to follow any of us home. He could be dangerous."

"We should stay here for a while, maybe he'll leave," suggested Kaila, getting up from her seat, taking Priscilla's hand and spinning her underneath her raised arm.

We continued our fun and paid him no attention almost forgetting he was there. Priscilla and Kaila left for the restroom and I sat with my head between my hands, elbows resting on the table.

Narrator

The man had been following them, although he was only interested in Sunshine, had been watching her every move, studying her. If she hadn't have been so plastered she would have felt his piercing, vicious eyes watching… watching. Club after club, he had been there, always watching. She sat down to get a grip on herself placing her delicate head between her hands. The world was spinning out of control around her. She could feel a nebulous repugnant force counteracting her luminous glow and felt that it was swallowing her whole. She looked up and saw him seated directly across from her at the table. She was no longer at the club. The music stopped and she could hear sounds from a radio, mingled with wind, and heavy rain. The man continued staring at her with his indignant eyes. From his lips uttered the word, "Delilah."

Sunshine

Suddenly, the room began to spin and I was somewhere else. The club had evaporated and I sat inside someone's house at their kitchen table. Across from me sat the man with his shifty eyes ogling me like I was his next casualty in a long line of them. The familiar sound of the tide beat against the sandy beach while the winds and rain waged a war outside. From beyond the house and the room, I heard a familiar voice call my name "Sunshine, Sunshine." He and the little house grew further away as my mind zoomed back to the here and now. No longer was he sitting across from me with his penetrating glare instead I was back in the club and he was gone. I stood and spun in circles, the bar was nearly empty and he had simply vanished. Priscilla, Kaila and my soon-to-be-mother-in-law surrounded me.

"I guess I've overdone the alcohol tonight," I blurted out, confused by the scene I had just witnessed.

"We all have," insisted Kaila.

"I'm almost ready for bed and Mr. Creepshow seems to be gone."

"We have one more stop planned for you. You ready?" Kaila asked.

The chaos inside my head wasn't completely gone, bits and pieces lingered. *Delilah.*

We piled back into the limo and headed to our final club destination. When we pulled up outside, the silhouette of a man flashed in brilliant green and blue lights that faded in and out and returned from his feet to his head. Inside was dark with strobe lights flickering every color of the rainbow. A spotlight surrounded the man on stage who was wearing nothing but a caveman thong around his middle as he gyrated his hips. A male strip club; no doubt a gag to accentuate my soon-to-be monogamous life. I wasn't a person who under ordinary terms would be caught dead in a strip club, but at this moment I welcomed it. I knew no self-respecting man would go into a male nudie club.

"What do you think?" whispered Priscilla in my ear as she leaned towards me.

"Classic," I responded with a laugh.

"You think he'll follow us in here?" I asked.

"Hell no!" was her hardy comeback. I felt safe in a manner of speaking. The men danced and tore off their clothes. They were very erotic and I couldn't believe my eyes. I couldn't fathom being in a place like this throwing money like the other women. They were bad, worse than men, jumping near the stage shoving money into the tiny G-strings that really didn't hide anything, and hollering at the tops of their lungs in high pitched wails. Until now I wasn't aware women could be such animals.

I scanned the room, taking a visual survey of the crowd that doubled as an observation of the female human savagery surrounding me and making sure Mr. Creepshow, as Kaila called him, wasn't present. Relief washed over me when I didn't spot his pinhead eyes watching me with his death glare.

My eyes detected someone, or rather something else, my apparition. Early this morning our moment had been interrupted, nevertheless now I had a second chance. My curiosity was now climaxing and I wanted to know, needed to know, who this woman was. In a hypnagogic state, I floated towards her. My body drifted without control from my mind, each step I took compelled by an internal motivation. My eyes locked onto her as I continued to drift towards her. The hollering, screaming and commotion inside the club faded until it was just the two of us. Her head bent down as always and dark tendrils of hair cascaded down her face and back.

The fear I normally felt was no longer present. Not wanting another interruption to halt our moment I quickly reached out my hand and touched her shoulder. I felt humanity and sorrow surge through my fingers where it rapidly coursed into my soul, and devastatingly hit my beating heart. *Thump, thump, thump…* a raging river of crimson blood flooded my vision as she lifted her slumped head. It poured down her body and puddled onto the floor around her originating from a laceration that extended across the full length of her neck.

Quiet words escaped from the small creases of her lips, "Remember." Her face I knew from long ago, from a time of innocence before night terrors controlled my dreams.

The power flickered and torrents of savage rain washed over the club beating down hard on the metal roof. I now stood facing a wall, my hand outstretched in the space where a few seconds ago my ghost had occupied. The world went back into its proper perspective as the pandemonium of sexually excited woman pounded my ears.

"What are you doing against the wall? You are drunk?" said Priscilla while stifling a laugh.

I'm sure it looked that way but my drunk had all but left me as I stood in the aftermath of my other worldly encounter.

"I'm ready to call it a night." I squeaked out in a barely audible tone.

"That's why I'm here, everyone else is already in the limo," she responded. The limo first dropped off Priscilla and Kaila at their hotel and drove my future mother-in-law and I back to Jerry's where he and his father would no doubt be waiting.

Monday

In less than a week, I would be married, Mrs. Jerry Butler, which meant I had a week to figure out the mystery that had encompassed my life for the past several weeks. *Remember, remember* echoed in my head. Remember what? The moment I touched her clarity festered to break the surface; it now teetered on the edge of my existence.

Buzz, buzz… went my phone. "Detective Henderson, good afternoon."

"I'm in Lyden, where would you like to meet?" He was always straight to the point.

"Across the street there is a bagel shop there." *The bagel shop is becoming a place of regular business for me. I almost need my own office*, I thought.

"Sounds good; I could use some coffee," he responded.

"Theirs is some of the best." I checked in with Joe and high-tailed it across the street where I ordered two coffees and waited.

Within fifteen minutes, Detective Henderson strolled through the door and instantly spotted me at a window booth. We dispensed with formalities and got to the meat of his visit.

Quietly, he leaned in, his comb over bobbing on the edge of his thick brows, "The evidence that was found was a pubic hair embedded in the back seat of her car. The team ran an analysis on it and it wasn't a match to hers. We ran it through the system and ping it matched an Evan O'Conner," he said with satisfaction.

I was confused, *who was Evan O'Conner?*

He continued, "When a person has been arrested, incarcerated or even put in the loony bin, information such as DNA and fingerprints is collected on them. This guy was never arrested but spent time in the loony bin when he was a kid from the time he was ten until eighteen years of age. At eighteen, they let him out."

A crazy guy, my mind buzzed with activity, "What did this guy do, why was he in a mental facility?" I asked.

"At age ten, his family; mom, dad, and little brother were brutally slaughtered. Somehow, he and his sister survived. She was two and placed into the foster system but he being older and displaying irrational behavior was placed into Windy Oaks Mental and Healthcare Center. At eighteen, they cut him loose saying he was mentally stable. He continued to receive outpatient services for the next two years. That's all I was able to get since he was a minor. The records are sealed and patient client confidentiality and all prevents anyone from divulging any more information."

I said my thoughts out loud, "So why would this guy's pubic hair be lying in the back seat of Eilida's car?"

"I asked the same question and that's the real reason that I'm here. I thought maybe she'd been raped, but her doctor says there was no sign of forced penetration; no bruising or lacerations in her vaginal area. They hadn't done a rape kit on her since there was no need to but the visual inspection of her body on arrival displayed no signs of rape."

"The woman who was murdered had been raped, right… post mortem you said?" Again, I was thinking out loud.

"Yes - and no semen had been found in her, on her or anywhere in the house. No evidence was found at the scene. So I keep asking why there was a pubic hair in her car?"

"It was planted!" I blurted out.

"You got it, pretty lady, but why?" He leaned back in the booth and sipped at his coffee.

"A vendetta, a crossed lover?" I suggested.

"Thought about that, but this guy's a loner and his record is squeaky clean. When a record is too clean, I question it, especially after this guy spent eight years of his childhood inside a state mental facility after witnessing the slaughter of his family."

"An angry victim," spilled off my tongue.

"It's possible. When a child witnesses the murder of his family, it's bound to leave some deep scars. His sister was probably too small to remember and she was found hidden inside a cabinet but he was old enough to remember," he replied.

I finally connected the dots within my mind, "The family in Chesterville they were all murdered by a knife across the throat, the mother had been raped and the youngest, a daughter, survived. Was his family murdered in the same fashion?" I questioned.

"Bingo!" busted forth from his lips. "My question is, did he commit the crime or is he being framed by the perp who killed his family?"

The question bobbing at the top of my brain was, *how old is this guy?* So I asked.

"He's thirty nine," he stated with no follow up.

"That would make the murderer of his family, what? About sixty, maybe seventy?" I asked.

"I got the same calculations - so either this guy is an agile old man or Evan is the guilty party. I hate to believe this guy could be guilty since he was a ten year old victim but it's the only thing that makes sense," he said with sorrow creasing the folds of his face.

He left and now I had more to ponder on, and a short time in which to solve it. My recent clairvoyance knew all this had something distinctive to do with me, or rather, with Eilida. My own research would prove nothing more than what Detective Henderson had revealed to me. I was left with no other choice but to make another appointment with Dr. Weered for Thursday afternoon. If the answer was hidden somewhere in my mind, I wanted the answers brought to the conscious part of it. Until then, Jerry and I had last minute wedding details to sort through.

Last Minute Details

Tuesday, during lunch, we made a trip to the caterers. Since the wedding and reception was happening at his parents' home we decided on an entire meal.

The gentleman in charge had a long oval face with round eyes and the bushiest eyebrows I had ever seen. They moved up and down with every word he spoke and resembled vermin. He was no taller than me and had a receding hairline that accentuated his already prolonged forehead. He greeted us with a faux hug and peck on both sides of our cheeks. He then took my right hand in both of his. For a short man I couldn't get over the size of his hands. They were huge and swallowed mine up.

"Mr. and Mrs. Butler," he said, as he cocked his huge head and raised his shoulder. "It's so exciting - such a beautiful young couple you make," he added, scrunching his nose and shortening his eyes which accentuated his elongated forehead even more. "We have a slight problem, although it won't be difficult to resolve. It had been unfortunate but we had to find a new crab and seafood supplier and it has been an arduous ordeal," he over emphasized arduous. "We found a new one who comes most highly recommended, but alas the shipment was no good. Huh… back to the drawing board." He said this finally letting go of my hand and placing his left one on his forehead. He shook his head in sorrow. I would say he was being a little melodramatic about seafood.

"Could we see the menu again and review the choices?" asked Jerry.

"Oh my, you will have to excuse my carelessness. Of course. Please take a seat and I will bring the menu to you." As he said this he looked genuinely in distress. We looked over the menu and decided on various cheeses, baguettes, an assortment of crackers; various thinly sliced meats, fresh fruit instead of the crab cakes, and the stuffed mushrooms we had previously chosen. The logic behind our choice was having a little something to wet everybody's taste buds. He adjusted the menu and offered us a ten percent discount due to our inconvenience. There was no doubt in my mind he was more stressed and inconvenienced over the crab affair than we were, although we graciously accepted the discount.

The entire meal consisted of a traditional yet bountiful assortment of foods and flavors. Subsequent to the appetizers we had a simple chopped salad with a creamy garlic sauce planned, followed up with baked rice, a roasted dish that included onions, asparagus, zucchini, tomato and eggplant. We also had a summer fruit salad made with a combination of cantaloupe and strawberries drizzled in a honey sauce with lime zest. The main course consisted of a choice between baked chicken and flank steak. The dessert, of course, would be wedding cake.

Wednesday, I rushed to Memories after work where I tried on my dress one last time before the wedding to make sure the alterations were correct. The dress fit like a dream. Tomorrow they would be delivering the dress to my soon-to-be-in-laws' house where it would be waiting for me on Saturday. In contrast, Jerry had made a dash to the Tux House. We had scheduled these the same day, planning to meet up for dinner afterwards.

As usual, Jerry was already waiting when I arrived at Manella's. He had already ordered spaghetti and meatballs for us and they were just bringing out our salad as I was seated. He leaned over and gave me a kiss. In just three days I would be his wife.

On the way home, I drove past the spot where my other worldly occurrence transpired the day I went dress shopping. I hadn't seen her face then due to the rain, darkness, and the fact that she had her head angled towards the ground. On the other hand, that night in the strip club I had seen her face clearly, and looked into her fathomless sapphire eyes and for that frozen moment in time I knew her. The reflections of my past and her importance in them disappeared when rain pounded the roof and the lights flickered, drawing me back into the present.

No, I Can't!

Thursday afternoon, my third session with Dr. Weered had rolled around. I wanted, more than ever, to recall the events that my conscious mind had worked over time for me to forget. Dr. Reisen wasn't present at the session. It was Dr. Weered, his medical assistant, and me.

Looking as furry as ever, he asked, "This session we are going back, as far back as you will allow yourself to go. I would like you to see and hear your actions, therefore I am asking to video record this."

I considered the value of his words and how watching myself may help to trigger some memories. On second thought, I was desperate and this needed to end today! I wanted to get married and start my new life in peace.

"Yes, you can." He handed me a form which I signed. He had a form for everything and my signature on more pieces of paper than I had signed the entire year.

Dr. Weered's soothing voice carried me back, back to the time when I was little and jumped into bed with my parents because of my nightmare.

"You're not alone; listen to my voice. I'm there with you. Let's go back to earlier in the day. What are you doing?"

"I'm in a swing near the lake with my Daddy."

"Use your senses and describe the area around you."

"The air is hot and wet and fish are swimming in the lake. I can see them when the swing goes high. There are birds too, and they look silly because of their really long necks."

"You're doing good, Eilida. Now, can you bring me back even further?" He asked.

"Mommy and me, my first mommy, we are looking out the window towards the beach. My first daddy is throwing a football and Ely catches it. Then he throws it, but not to daddy, he throws it to Evie. Evie doesn't catch it so he runs into the tide and water splashes all over him. He looks funny," I laugh. "A man, he picks up the ball and hands it to Evie. The man, he… AHHHHH" I screamed.

A screeching sound felt as if it was drilling a hole in my head and I couldn't see the man or anyone anymore. I saw blackness instead. My head was in excruciating pain. "Eilida, follow my voice. On the count of

three you will return to my office, one…
two… three…"

My brain no longer felt as though it was
being crushed and the piercing noise had
disappeared. When I first opened my eyes, I
saw the black leather couch and my body was
scrunched into the fetal position with my butt
high in the air. My hands surrounded my
head, which was buried into the couch.

I asked myself, "How did I get into this
position?"

It was one of those questions I accidently
said out loud and he responded, "You saw a
man hand Evie a ball and your hands
suddenly pressed against your skull and you
twisted around on the couch ending up in that
position." As he spoke, I readjusted myself
until I was sitting vertically on the couch.

"Evie, who is that?" I asked out loud on
purpose.

He responded in a questioning tone, "I
was hoping you could tell me?"

"I don't remember." I answered. The
name seemed significant. Like a ton of bricks
falling from a ten story roof against my skull, I
suddenly remembered.

"Evie, that's one of Jay's roommates."

"I assume Jay is a friend of yours?" He
asked. I had neglected to tell Dr. Weered
about Jay because of our little affair. Jay
thinking I was Eilida and my playing along.

"A little. He is Eilida's boyfriend and I met him because he thought I was her," I said hesitantly.

"Let's watch the video, are you ready to do that?" I felt relief wash over my body as he didn't ask any more about the situation.

"I think so," I responded.

"I need a yes or no answer from you," he insisted.

I took a deep breath, "Yes."

In the video, I talked and sounded like a little girl. I made childlike faces, freaky. *My first mommy and daddy?* I questioned inside my head this time. Ely and Evie were both present tossing a ball with my daddy? *Were they kids? Had I known them as children?* In my recollections, as Dr. Weered called them, I was very little, just a baby. Detective Burkhalder had told me Eilida's parents and family had been killed during Hurricane Chloe. These were her parents and mine. *Is that what she withheld?*

We both survived but were separated after the deaths of our parents. Burkhalder said *unfinished business.* I couldn't help but wonder; *was I part of that unfinished business?* Was that her true reason in talking with me? When we got to the beach scene my body did just as he described. I grabbed my head and buried myself while screaming like I was in paralyzing pain.

When the movie was over, Dr. Weered looked at me through the fuzz that covered most of his face wearing an unmistakable solemn expression. Then, he spoke, "You have to be honest with me if we are going to figure this out." He was right, I knew that. It was time to tell him more.

I asserted, "I think they are my brothers. I talked with a detective the other day. She grew up with my…" I thought about that for a second, then I continued, "*Our* father. A hurricane killed our family. Eilida went to live with her… *our* aunt and uncle and me…" I searched my head some more and went on, "I was put up for adoption."

"She told you this?" he asked, there was a horrified look in his eyes.

"No, she only spoke of Eilida… but if I'm her twin..." I was over reaching and assuming, however it made sense, "I didn't go live with her so I ended up being adopted. Maybe they couldn't take on two kids?"

"Did she specify that Eilida had a twin?"

"No, I wasn't part of the story at all but we are identical and I remember everything as if I was Eilida. I've done enough research on twins to know that's possible." I said matter of factly.

He took a minute and considered what I said, then stated, "I don't think you are her twin."

I was outraged, "Not her twin?! Two children born on the same day who are identical in appearance except for one aspect, our hair, not twins?" *What planet did he live on?*

"I have been in the business of hypnosis since you were a baby. Your recollections are too precise."

"Then, who am I if not her twin?"

His eyes searched my face while he said, "Are you ready?"

Ready for what, wolf man hypnologic? I wondered angrily but, I responded with, "Yes, I am ready."

"You are Eilida."

He was full of shit! She was in a hospital bed and I was here with him in his grotesquely decorated office. I stood, grabbed my purse and stomped out the door.

Eilida

My breakthroughs within the structure of my memories continued their onslaught of information. One minute my dad was swinging me and the next I was even younger and watching my dad out of the window, only he wasn't the dad I knew. The one that visited me daily in the hospital, instead he was the dad I remembered with faint jagged images, my dad from long ago. My mother held me tight as we watched out the window.

I had seen this vision in the past, my dad throwing a football to two little boys who I now knew were my brothers. Ely overthrew the ball to Evie where it bobbled along the front of the tide, slowly rolling in and out. A man walking on the beach picked up the ball and handed it to him. His beady black eyes looked towards the window and threatened to swipe my essence clean away from me.

The Wedding Must Go On

Sunshine

When Friday came, instead of work we drove to Jerry's parents' home. We had a rehearsal dinner planned at El Fin Está Cerca, which was an exclusive Hispanic restaurant. It was an elegant establishment with collections of carnations and roses brimming from every corner. Plush gold velvet chairs surrounded glass tables which supported more roses and carnations. Paintings of Spain's countryside scattered Sangria red walls which began to drip blood that puddled underneath, soon a river of blood washed over the floor. It was everywhere and small branches streamed around me until I was encircled by them.

"This way," said Jerry's father as he took my hand. The blood receded back into the walls.

Several tables had been pushed together in order to accommodate the entire wedding party which consisted of Jerry and I, his parents, my bridesmaids and his groomsman and best man.

The menu had already been chosen by my soon-to-be-in-laws and our first snack was tapas as everyone arrived. The appetizer was followed by roasted fish, various vegetables, chorizo, and rice finished with flan as dessert. The food smelled savory but my taste buds had gone sour after envisioning all the blood. I dared not look at the walls in fear of what my mind's eye would perceive. Instead, I chose to drink.

A delicious Cabernet Sauvignon had been delivered and the server went around the table filling our glasses. She then left the bottle within reach of me and opened two others setting one at the other end and one in the middle, all chilling on ice. I picked at my meal, drank several glasses of wine and felt tanked by the time we left.

During the entire ride to their house my head was spinning and I was so glad no food was in my belly or I would have regurgitated it back up. Inside their mansion the spiral staircase loomed before me. I stumbled up the stairs with Jerry's mom holding onto me the entire length.

"You have to watch that wine, it tastes so good and before you know it you're drunk." She said, as we maneuvered the stairs. Immediately, I went to the right because the room I normally stayed in was that direction. She held my arm and redirected me, "Not tonight. You will stay in a special room that I have prepared for you."

The room was huge with a queen four poster bed caught in the middle. She opened my suitcase and muddled around until she found a nightgown then she placed it on the bed, where I was now sitting. "Do you need help with this, sweetie?" she asked. I now saw two of her and nodded my head yes.

I was drawn back in time and now too young to dress myself. "Mommy?" The words floundered off my lips and hung in the air.

"Sleep baby, you need your rest," she said quietly, leaving the room.

From the closet, I spied my wedding dress through a small sliver where the door didn't meet the frame. With exaggerated movements I walked to the closet, almost falling into the broad door, catching my balance against the wall. I pushed against the door and my magnolia white wedding gown hung on a mannequin in front of me. I caressed it with my fingers. It was immaculate and pristine; tomorrow I would be Mrs. Jerry Butler.

I was too exhausted from the evening and several glasses of wine to admire it anymore tonight so I bobbled back to the bed, crawled under the covers and fell into a hard sleep. Thunder rumbled above my head, a sharp crack of lightning lit up the room. The rain outside came down in unyielding torrents. I was too tired and inebriated for fear.

In my dream, I touched the bathroom mirror and my dark haired ghost stood on the other side looking back at me. Her eyes were wells deep and sorrowful. Tears began to run down her cheeks and then the tears turned to blood that poured down her face and onto her neck where more blood flowed from the wedge across it.

Abruptly, she was gone and fragmented images took her place. A young, tall gangly man with wispy thin straight hair hands me a monkey and says, "Its over." Then, he is gone and I'm a little child. My apparition is holding me, singing, but I hear no words.

Still a small child; I'm inside a box, no a wooden chest, hiding inside it and the monkey is with me. The chest lid opens and two young boys, Ely and Evie, are laughing and teasing. Ely, the older of the two boys puts him arms around my middle and lifts me and the monkey out of the chest, I'm giggling. The image fades and I'm at a table with my parents and the two boys, my brothers.

An evil man is there glaring at me through small black pits and a vile agony clutches at my heart. Tears flood my eyes and flow down my chubby baby cheeks. Outside, the wind is raging and rain is hammering down on the house. The room is dark except a few candles whose glow lights up the blackness surrounding them. Behind the man, a villainous shadow holding a pointed blade dances across the wall. Against the charcoal air the blade turns silver and pools of red discharge from its sharp tip.

Drop, drop, drop… droplets of crimson blood fill the carpet and I'm no longer in my mother's arms, we are no longer at the table. I am alone inside the chest and I can hear lumbering footsteps coming closer. I hug my monkey…

Beep, beep, beep… my alarm sounded, jolting me from the dream, from my recollections. My head was wrapped in fabric which I beat off me in a panic. *Thunk!* My wedding dress, mannequin and all, fell to the floor. The comforter from the bed was cloaked around me. What the hell was I doing in the closet? A bombshell blasts in my head and I remember the last time I visited I woke up in a closet as well.

The bedroom door creaked open and in ran Jerry's father. His eye brows munched and wrinkles crept across his receding bald head, "What the…" He began to say but I finished his sentence.

"I tripped but I'm alright."

"Allow me to give you a hand," he offered, helping my pitiful self off the floor.

I'm sure this situation looked awfully strange to him. "I don't think the dress is injured either," I responded as we picked up and inspected the mannequin.

He looked at me odd, then says, "Breakfast should be ready in ten minutes."

Breakfast consisted of crepes filled with strawberries. My appetite was voracious and I swallowed down three along with a cup of orange juice. My head throbbed from mollycoddling too much wine the previous night.

After breakfast came the beauty crews in waves. My nails and toes were operated on first. The pedicure and manicure were just what the doctor ordered and the thumping in my head dulled until a dim intermittent pain thumbed against my temples. When my fingers and toes had passed inspection I received a facial. Warm scents blasted my nostrils as she applied a cucumber mint masque followed by a fruity cleanse and topped off with a jasmine scented moisturizer.

Next was lunch, which consisted of spinach, bacon quiche, fresh watermelon and grapes along with a full twelve ounce bottle of water. By this time the hair dresser had arrived. My headache had completely disappeared as he massaged my hair then washed and conditioned it, leaving on a hot towel before rinsing. He then blow dried it and styled it into a bun leaving a few stray ringlets throughout the nape of my neck and forehead.

Priscilla and Kaila had shown during lunch and were given a similar hair treatment as me. We gathered around as they and Jerry's mom assisted me into my gown. When all was done I looked into the mirror and smoothed my dress. It fit like a glove around my frame.

My soon-to-be-mother-in-law gasped, "You make a stunning bride. Jerry will be so pleased when he sees you."

"Thank you."

I blushed, although I had to admit I was flabbergasted at my own reflection in the mirror.

While I was being whooshed around Jerry was in another room on the other side of the house being prepped. We were being given the royal treatment as though we were King and Queen. According to the old wives tale, it would bring bad luck if the groom were to see the bride before the wedding, which is why we were on opposite sides of the house. As much pampering as I had received, my mind wasn't into the wedding. Visions of my dream swarmed in and out of my mind. As the day passed, all that was left was fragmented jagged images.

From downstairs, I could hear the wedding march begin and my very-soon-to-be-father-in-law took my arm, escorting me down the spiral stairs, my dress flowed behind us. The moment seemed perfect and even though he wasn't my father, he felt like he was, if just for the moment.

Jerry stood at the altar; his chestnut hair glistening from the lighting above, a cream tux and yellow cummerbund accentuated his frame. Mr. Butler deposited me next to Jerry who wore a smile across his handsome face.

We recited our vows and a peaceful feeling enveloped me.

His best man's son played the part of ring bearer, wearing a tux similar to Jerry's. On a cream pillow, Jerry carefully unwound the satin bow holding the ring and eased it on my finger. He then lifted my veil and we kissed. I was now Mrs. Jerry Butler. Our union symbolized the beginning of our new life; the life we would share together for better or for worse.

The reception immediately followed the ceremony. For the first hour, the entire wedding party was whisked away for pictures. When we returned to the celebration, the caterers were just beginning to serve the food which turned out wonderful. Jerry's parents made us a toast and his father invited me to a father - daughter dance. Cameras flashed throughout the course of it. I had had so many pictures taken of me, colors swirled in my eyes when I blinked.

The best man and my bridesmaids - I hadn't singled one out to be a maid of honor - toasted us with champagne and we cut the cake. We danced under the stars with lightning bugs twinkling in the bushes until one by one our guests began to leave. It was then all the young ladies were gathered together as I tossed my bouquet. My life at that moment was perfect and I felt as though it would last forever. It was like being stuck inside a wonderful, never ending fantasy.

Our bags were already packed and waiting in the car. After the father - daughter dance, I had changed my clothes into a loose skirt and blouse. I really wanted jeans and a T-shirt, but something inside said that would be *inappropriate*.

For our departing honeymoon gift, his father gave us a small box which Jerry handed me to open. Inside it was a silver key. His father winked and said, "Might as well spend the weekend at the beach house before leaving on the cruise Monday." His mother eked out a simple smile and waved as we pulled out of the drive.

Hurricane

"**D**idn't you say their beach house was in Billows Hollow?" I asked as we sailed down the road.

"It is," Jerry replied.

My mind was now spinning. We were spending the weekend in Billows Hollow exactly twenty one years after Hurricane Chloe? That couldn't be good, nor could it be a coincidence. I slid my phone out of my purse and checked my weather app. I typed in Billows Hollow and the weather looked clear for the weekend with a possible disturbance by late Monday evening, but we would be gone by then.

"Who are you texting?" he asked.

"No one, I was just turning it off." I lied, but he had never believed any of my paranormal craziness and I didn't want to spoil the mood. Instead, I eased the chair back and played with the radio until I found a station with soft rock.

Three hours later, I could see the coast wash up along the sandy beach. Excitement and fear swelled inside me as a bout of déjà vu told me I had been here. I was home. He opened my car door and we walked around the side of the house to the back where I could see the beach.

The tide was rolling in and out leaving ripples in the sand beneath it. Ely and Evie ran through the water splashing and laughing while my mother and father chased after them.

"Sunshine?" Questioned Jerry. "You were lost in your own world for a second. I asked if you could give me a hand."

Confused, I strolled to the door beside him and he lifted me up and carried me over the threshold. I leaned in and gave him a kiss.

Jerry carried me all the way to the bedroom where he kissed and caressed my body while removing every stitch of my clothing. We made love and I remembered Jay with his straight teeth that compelled me to jump inside his mouth and the sway of our naked bodies as they melded together.

Inside, I knew every detail of the house, it was uncanny. The room I now lay in making love with my husband held comfort and horror in the deep recesses of my mind. It had once been a pale green and now was nothing more than a common white. I closed my eyes and tried to forget about losing my virginity to Jay and this house, and concentrate on my husband who thought he was the first to give me this pleasure.

When I opened my eyes, I didn't see Jerry but the bald tiny black eyed man staring down at me, "Delilah," sputtered from his mouth, and I used all the strength in my muscles to cast him off me.

When I looked again, Jerry was lying beside me dumbfounded.

"I'm so sorry," I muttered, feeling like a complete idiot.

"If you're not ready or I've done something wrong…"

I put my finger to his mouth as if to say be quiet and whispered. "I love you, Jerry Butler."

We went for a late night stroll along the beach. The waters were calm and the sky was clear but that was little comfort as I had a feeling growing inside me, doom - something I couldn't explain, couldn't wrap my mind around. I didn't know how to deal with what I felt. So much had happened in the last couple months and fear had overcome me more than once, but the feeling in my gut now was something worse, and more than fear.

Jerry went right to sleep after our walk. My mind raced like the Indie 500 and sleep did not visit me. I arose, and padded to the kitchen for water. My purse lay on the table and a paper creased the top. Gently, I pulled it out, barely remembering what it could be.

As I unfolded it, I realized it was some of the research I had done on Hurricane Chloe. I smoothed it out and began to read… A two year old girl was found in the innermost room and the only part of her family's house still standing. Her parents' closet, the innermost room. She was hidden inside a wooden *chest.* Chills engulfed me from head to toe but still I read on… *One of the rescue workers heard her muffled cries... Both her parents and two brothers were killed in the storm. Their deaths may have been foul play.*

What kind of foul play? And how did they know this? I began to wonder. *In all the pictures I've seen the entire beach front was wiped out. The article said nothing about a sister because Dr. Weered had been right, she had no sister.*

Eilida

I was sent to live with my aunt and uncle after the hurricane. They are the people who I know as my parents, the ones who raised a broken, devastated little girl. The room around me suddenly brightened and the *beep, beep, beep* of my heart monitor became sharper and the pain resurfaced. A concert of emotions and vivid dreams danced around inside my head and I was completely cognizant and aware of my surroundings, and the pain…

Sunshine

I slunk back into bed and lay beside my husband, my head resting against his chest, moving up and down with each breath he took. My tired eyes and body eventually gave in to sleep.

When I woke the following morning, Jerry had already made coffee. The aroma wafted through the house. He was sitting on the back porch watching the ocean. The house sat high on the shore overlooking the sand and waves. I grabbed a mug of coffee and joined him outside, planting myself in one of the wicker chairs resting diagonally to his, everything was quiet and serene. A gentle steady breeze controlled the morning air.

After our coffee, we went for another walk along the beach with our feet in the water. The day was classic and small children and their parents began to dot the beach, packing with them umbrellas and coolers.

I had weathered the anniversary of Hurricane Chloe in Billows Hollow and was still standing. No evil force had taken me down and the day was too perfect to believe it would. My repressed memories hadn't been mine, they were Eilida's. Somehow, she had communicated telepathically with me from beyond her bed.

I pulled my phone out and checked the weather app. The tropical disturbance off the coast was traveling faster, and the winds had reached hurricane strength, the eye was clearly defined. It was projected to make landfall several miles to the south of us. At the current rate it was moving, the storm would hit by next morning.

The beach held its secrets and showed no signs. It was the calm before the storm. All the pieces were beginning to fit together. I quickly shoved my phone back in my purse as Jerry entered the room. I didn't dare tell him about the disturbance as he would accuse me of overreacting.

For dinner, we made a salad and cooked spaghetti with garlic bread and Jerry brought out some wine. We ate, drank, and laughed, followed by consummating our marriage again; although this time I didn't see the frightening man, all I saw was Jerry.

Sex wore him out and he slept like an infant. I slipped out of bed and tiptoed down the hallway to another bedroom. I knew this house, from somewhere inside my fragmented head, and the room I was entering. I couldn't place how I did but I knew it. The furniture was different and the walls were painted, but a faint outline of a palm tree and monkeys showed through. I traced each curve of their outline.

Eilida

Agony reached every possible muscle in my body as I attempted to lift myself upwards. Slowly I edged forward from the pillow that supported my back only to fall onto it once again. A storm raged in my head and images whirled like a cyclone through it. Outside the window, redbuds swayed with the ocean breeze until darkness covered it like a plague. Ughh… I squeezed my eyes, allowing my memory to convulse and consume me.

The room shifted frames in front of my eyes, and suddenly I'm two and lying in my crib. My brothers, Ely and Evie, are fast asleep in the room beside mine. I can hear my parents talking in the living room with the stranger. But I can't sleep, my room is too dark, and branches slam hard against the walls outside. The stranger chuckles stiffly as if he's being forced.

A crash slammed into my window, scaring me. I wrapped my hands around Sandy, my stuffed monkey, and curled my body into a ball. Nimble footsteps came down the hall and a dim light shone beneath my door; mommy poked her head in, "Baby, why don't you sleep with us? I don't like the storm either but your brothers - they could sleep through anything." She said plucking me out of my crib and wiggling her nose to mine. "I love you," she planted a kiss on my left cheek. I folded myself into the nape of her neck.

Daddy walked out of my brothers' room, "Those boys are sound asleep and the plywood seems to be holding up. I'm going to set my alarm and check on them in a couple hours."

"This little one here is the insomniac," said my mommy.

He leaned over and gave me a kiss, "She doesn't like the rain, do you, hon?" I tilted my head upwards and reached out my arm attempting to grab his nose. I snuggled between my parents and dozed off to sleep.

It wasn't long before I heard the stranger sauntering around the house with his heavy feet. *Clunk, clunk, clunk* through the hallway, lingering for a second in front of my door. Then a loud creak told me he was in my brothers' room. "Mommy, Daddy," I whispered nudging them but they wouldn't wake up.

Loud thumping footsteps echoed down the hall towards my parents' room and terror gripped me. Suddenly, I felt alone in the house with him. "Mommy, daddy," I whispered once more and then, I scuttled off the bed, with Sandy in tow.

Loud crashes hit the house from the outside as me and Sandy scurried to the closet where I hid between mommy's dresses. The bedroom door opened with its familiar groan and his pounding footsteps walked towards my parents' bed. A flashlight in his hand illuminated the room and I squished further back into the closet. His heavy hand rested his flashlight upon the tall dresser beside the window.

The stranger was soon by my daddy's side, in his hand a slender, shiny object. The object glistened from the light as the stranger slid it across Daddy's neck. Red flowed like a heavy river. He wasted no time in running the object across my mommy's neck, red flowed around her too. Then, he pulled down his pants and forced my mommy's nightgown upwards exposing her bare legs and belly. The light from the dresser acted like a spotlight framing his every move.

"Mommy," I uttered in barely a whisper while he removed a shiny package from his pocket and opened it up. His wide body lumbered on top of mommy and he lingered there bouncing on top of her for several minutes. A large growl like that of a dog emerged from his lips, emanating from somewhere deep and dark inside him. I hoped Mommy kneed him and that it was a growl of pain.

His head drifted towards her ear and he whispered something out of my earshot. He slipped off her and left her lying in bed motionless; light streaming across her near naked and bloody body. *Daddy why did you let him hurt her? Why didn't she scream to wake up Daddy?* My young brain was too small to comprehend.

Hurriedly, he pulled his pants back on and shined the flashlight across the room and into the closet, "Where are you... I'll find you," he ridiculed. The light from his flashlight glowed into the closet, the stranger stood next to me. We were separated only by mommy's dresses. I crawled as far back in the closet as I could. Fabric covered my vision but I knew he was there, I could hear him panting and smell his sweat - putrid and musky.

He shifted his bulk and moved away from the closet. Throughout the house, his heavy menacing footfalls traipsed in and out of every room, followed with, "A little girl can hide in many places but you can't hide from me forever."

I hadn't moved from my spot in the closet except to breathe. After a long time, the front door slammed shut and I closed my eyes, holding Sandy between my chest and the floor. Silence filled the air and I realized the rain had stopped and I no longer heard his heavy footsteps. Paralyzed with fear that he would return, I stayed hidden in the closet.

I waited and when I hadn't heard his foot falls or his taunting voice for what felt like hours, I crawled out of my hiding spot and over to my parents' bed where I climbed up to join them. Their necks were severed and blood was puddled everywhere in the bed, like a swamp only it was red and sticky. All my two year old brain could think was *maybe if I bandaged them they would be OK and wake up...* Whenever I got hurt and bled, my parents put bandages on my boo-boos. From under the bathroom sink, I pulled out all the bandages I could carry, and wrapped them around my parents.

What about my brothers? He had been in their room, too. I had mustered all the courage that a two year old with tears flooding down her face could and went into their room. Shadow lumps in their bed told me they were in them. The placid silence told me the man had hurt them, too. I tried to wake them up but they wouldn't. Sticky viscous wetness clung to their sheets and my clothes. I used the rest of the bandages to cocoon their wounds. *They should all be OK now*, but still no one moved.

I wanted to lie in bed with Mommy and Daddy but it was too gluey, so I cuddled Sandy to me and we climbed into the wooden chest in my parents' closet. When I played hide and seek I always hid there, and eventually someone found me. I decided that when Mommy and Daddy, Ely, and Evie (short for Evander, but Mommy and Daddy only called him that when he was in trouble) are feeling better they would find me and we'd play. Mommy kept the chest empty because it was my favorite hiding spot. She also left me little snacks and juice boxes as surprises.

Daddy drilled holes in the sides so I could see out. He called them 'peep holes'. Inside the chest I waited and waited. I could hear the storm again, outside. I heard stuff, big things hitting the house, and it sounded as though it was being ripped to pieces. The wind was much louder and closer than before. It was too dark to see anything from my peep holes but it sounded like I was in the middle of all the wind and rain, just Sandy and I. Snuggling Sandy closer than ever I tried to go to sleep so Mommy and Daddy or one of my brothers would find me. They always did. I shut my eyes and we slept.

Awake

"Eilida, Eilida!" called an ubiquitous voice. "Get the doctor!" Within seconds, bold lights flashed into my eyes and a hairy face was staring at me.

"I'm going to have to ask you to step out for a few moments until we can examine her," commanded a voice from afar.

"Eilida," said a gentle male voice, "Do you know where you are?" Mind tremors took me in and out of the present like ferocious waves. *You can't hide from me* sounded against my cranium.

"You're in the hospital. I'm Doctor Wolfgang Weered. You have been here for nine days…" His voice droned on in a calm soothing manner from under the bushels of hair that covered his face.

The room around me repositioned itself as my vision cleared. "The hospital… I fell. I was running…"

"Don't push too hard, take your time. Your family is in the other room and would like to see you."

Perched outside the door was a uniformed police officer. I had to tell the story. My arm hurt like a bitch but I managed to lift it enough to point, "Him, can you get me him?" Dr. Weered followed my hand with his eyes.

The officer, hearing my request, looked at the doctor who gave him a nod of approval.

He was young; somewhere in his twenties with blond hair styled in a high and tight.

"Ma'am," he said, standing beside my bed.

"I remember, can you get me De - tec - tive He - enderson," the name sounded right but I had a difficult time finding the words.

"Yes ma'am," and he pulled out his phone and walked towards the door. "She's awake and asking for you." He hung up the phone and marched back to my bedside, "He's on his way," then, he reposted himself to my doorway.

My family came in and gathered around me with tears of joy and showered me with kisses and hugs.

"You have been in a coma for a week. I was so scared that you might not wake up, but here you are. I love you, honey," said my mom with tears of happiness drizzling down her cheeks. She wrapped her arms tight around me as if she would never see me again.

I wanted my family, my aunt and uncle, the only parents I had ever really known. They had loved me like their own daughter and

Sage, having no siblings of my own that I could ever remember, was like my sister.

"Lida, love you Babe," said Sage as she crawled into bed beside me like old times when we were small children.

I turned towards my parents, "I remember all of it, my parents, Ely, Evie, and the storm. I know what happened to them. I was there… I saw it," I said, my words now able to find my voice and my voice unable to stop.

"Honey, you don't have to think about it now," interupted my father.

"I do and the Turnwell family. I saw them, too. The detective, I heard her, she said you were in denial. She meant me, because you never told me."

"How could we? You were two years old. You needed to be safe and loved." My mom pleaded with me. She then paused for a moment, her waterlogged eyes boring into mine, "You heard that conversation?"

"Yes! I've heard everything since I've been here and I'm not two anymore. I have an officer posted outside my door." I replied with my still shaky voice.

My parents looked at each other and then me with blank stares for several seconds as they processed all that I had told them.

"We should have told you when you were old enough to understand but a parent never wants anything horrible to happen to their child," my dad's eyes filled with sorrow.

"I love you," I replied with my arms outstretched. I would always love them. "Detective Henderson will be here soon and I'm going to tell him everything, all of it."

The Turnwells

Within the hour, Det. Henderson had arrived. I poured into my story with little to no formalities. He seemed willing to listen. "The dark clouds hovered over my head telling me it would be storming soon. I thought I should be able to get off the mountain and into town before it got too bad. I could always stay with a friend if necessary instead of going back home. At some point in my life, I will have to face storms and stop being such a pussy. I have never liked them as long as I can recall and I won't drive in them but the storm was still off in the distance," I grimaced.

He sat intently as I went on. "As I stepped into my car, I noticed all the lights were off at the Turnwells' except for a dim light in the back of their house. I thought that was odd. They were a routine family and should have been in the living room watching movies. It was a Friday night and that was their usual family routine. They called it 'family time'. The boys were older and sometimes, they stayed with friends on Friday nights but still, Mr. and Mrs. Turnwell and their daughter would have been home. I had seen the lights on earlier and a shadow passed in front of the window. The shadow looked different, short, stocky and devoid of hair. It triggered an image from a time I couldn't remember, like a flashback of some sort, a bald man with shadows dancing on the wall behind him. It was peculiar…" my mind lingered for a moment.

Det. Henderson's eyes hung on every word I spoke.

"When you live on a mountain in the woods with few people around, you get familiar with your neighbors' routines and their shadows; it's like a sixth human sense. Living out there brings one closer and more alert to their surroundings. My sixth sense took over and the storm no longer intimidated me. Gently, I closed my car door and quickly and quietly stole across the gravel road. I put my ear next to the house and listened intently. I could hear the little girl crying softly. I wrapped my body into the fabric of the house and moved like a ninja sliding along the outside of the house. He didn't belong there, yet I knew I had seen him before. Somewhere in my life, he had brought evil."

Repugnant, vile, and eerie the memory lay on the plane between my conscious and subconscious; penetrating deep into the folds of my brain… Deep beyond, in a place I couldn't reach, a place that was black and red;

crimson red everywhere. It flowed like an unforgiving river and it was sticky and gooey.

"As I reached the steps leading up to the back deck, out of instinct, I stopped and looked. I could barely see, but I could still hear the girl and her gentle wails as she cried for her Mommy and Daddy. My body stole up the steps but what I saw when I got to the top was unfathomable. Mr. and Mrs. Turnwell were lying motionless on the floor, their necks slit and covered in sticky blood. Lakes of red oozed around their necks and heads. The little girl was crying softly beside them, trying to wake them up and the boys were propped in chairs, their necks wearing identical lacerations. Rivers of blood had flowed down their bodies and pooled onto the floor beneath them. My head became flooded with memories and my body, working on a sixth sense and adrenaline, ran." It was hard to finish sharing the memory, but I had to.

"When I was a baby, I witnessed the murder of my own parents and lay in a pool of their blood, much like the Turnwell girl did. I didn't know where I was going but I had to go somewhere, anywhere but there."

Memories of my parents lying motionless in bed submerged my brain. Mentally, I switched gears and was a child. "The bandages didn't bring them back. Ely and Evie, Mommy, and Daddy never found me but how could they? They were dead, dead!

Their necks were bathed in their own blood. No simple bandage could stop the flow and it was too late! When short, stocky, and bald had slid the sharp knife across their necks, it was over! The storm beating on the little house was not as scary as what was inside. The chest! I was inside the chest with Sandy, my monkey Sandy. We waited for them to feel better and find us, but dead people don't find anybody! I was in the chest eating the cookies and drinking the juice boxes Mommy had hidden in there. I could see daylight through the peep holes but I didn't get out. I could hear sounds of someone walking around. I don't know how long I was in the chest, maybe days, maybe hours… but it seemed like an eternity before someone found us…"

He seemed to interpret my childlike voice as a cue that my brain was working too hard, "We don't have to finish today."

I sighed and continued, "I do. For me I do. When the lid to the chest opened up, there was sunshine everywhere and my parents' bedroom door was open. The daylight was pouring through what used to be the roof and the walls. Some of the walls were missing. 'Oh Delilah, Oh Delilah, Oh my darling, Deli-lah you were gone and lost forever, oh my De-Li-i-a-lah' he sang to the tune of Clementine. 'They named you wrong, you little devious bitch.'".

I paused for a second to catch my breath and keep the flood gates that threatened my eyes closed before going on. "His words reverberated inside of me, 'Delilah.' He lifted me out. His piercing black eyes penetrated inside me like a laser beam. I didn't want him to touch me so I cried as loud as I could.

"My parents were covered in wood and glass. I could barely see them underneath the rubble except my Mommy's black hair flowing from the side of the bed. The stranger talked to me while I cried. 'You are clever, little Delilah, hiding in a wooden chest. I looked for you and here you are. I figured I would leave you to the storm. How could a little thing like you live through something so fierce? But yet, here you are. And it looks like you have been busy. You found your Mommy and Daddy. You have their blood all over you. And what is this you are holding onto, a monkey? Well, it looks like I will have to hand you over, but the monkey is mine. It is my souvenir.' said the stranger, mockingly while viewing something behind me. It was only seconds later when I heard footfalls and a female voice.

"Detective Burkhalder found us and saved me from him, only she had no idea he was a killer. She must have assumed he was a citizen helping with search and rescue efforts. I stopped crying but I wanted Mommy and Daddy, Ely, and Evie. They were supposed to find me; them… not him. I wanted Sandy, too. Sandy was my only family left and I wanted Sandy but he had Sandy. The woman took me to a large building with lots of other people who had wounds but not as bad as my parents'.

"I stayed in the big building for days while doctors looked at me and said I was healthy, although a bit undernourished. I guess snacks and juice boxes don't provide a balanced diet." I joked, more to calm myself than Det. Henderson, who sat still as a stone. "They also said how hiding in the chest is probably what saved my life. The rest of my house was destroyed. They said, 'Your aunt and uncle will be picking you up and you will be living with them'.

"I had met them before, my aunt and uncle. They had stayed with us but I barely remembered them. Mostly, I knew them by pictures. I liked to look at pictures, and Mommy would show me pictures and tell me about the people in them, so I knew he was Mommy's brother. She had told me stories about her brother. He was just like Mommy described, and my aunt and uncle loved me and took me far away from my home, from the stocky bald man, from my family and Sandy," For those brief moments, I was a lost little child again.

"Finally, the detective had something to say, "You're telling me the same guy killed the

Turnwells', forgive the harsh words, killed your family, too?" he leaned forward in the chair, his donut gut hanging grossly over his belt; he smashed his caterpillar-bush eyebrows together and contemplated all that I had told him.

"That is exactly what I'm telling you. I saw him and I'm positive it's the same guy." I wanted my family's memory consecrated and their murderer wiped off the face of the planet. I didn't feel hurt anymore but anger.

He scratched his head for a minute, his top wisps of hair now saluting from static electricity then asked, "You think you could give us a sketch?"

"I know I could!"

"I'm not going to candy coat it, you were a baby and at your neighbors, all you saw was his shadow. This type of evidence doesn't always hold up, but I will accept your help. You are the only lead we got. No DNA or fingerprints showed up at the scene. Forensics did uh… they pulled a hair from your car."

I could hear the hesitation in his voice. Coma or not for several days I could handle it, "His?" I questioned knowing damn well the answer.

"We don't know yet. I got a name and photo. I pulled his record and he's clean but the hair was in your car and you didn't drive it that night. Somebody did and it turned up in the woods outside of Salvation Cove." His tone suggested he was waiting for my response.

I thought back for a minute, mentally retracing my steps. "I had my keys with me. I stepped out of my car and they were still in my hand. I'm sure of it. They landed somewhere on that mountain!" A thought suddenly beamed into my brain, "You said you have an ID and a picture?"

He smiled, that's what he was waiting for. From inside his jacket pocket he pulled out a small notepad, opened it up and withdrew a picture. "You sure you're ready, you've been in a coma for nearly a week?"

After telling him a story my memory had repressed since I was two I felt ready for anything, almost. "Yes, no, yes, I may never be more ready than I am now, and there is only one way to know. I need to see it."

He handed me the picture and I didn't need to study it, immediately I knew whether or not it was the same guy. He had haunted me for twenty one years in my night terrors. "That's him. What is his name?"

"I can't tell you that yet, but I thank you for your help, pretty lady. I'll be back." He tilted his head and left.

Who do I Thank?

My family, Sage, and now Jay, sat quietly in my room as I relayed my gruesome memoirs to Det. Henderson. Jay had just arrived as I was finishing. It was Sage that texted him upon my waking up. After Detective Henderson left, my parents and friends filled in the gaps. I had been found approximately twenty-four hours after the incident by an unknown individual who apparently called 911.

During my first forty-eight hours in the hospital, I was placed in the critical care area. My wounds had become infected and my body ran a fever for nearly two days. During that time, I was awake, although completely delirious and apparently made no sense as I ranted and raved about sunshine.

When my fever started to clear, and the doctors believed me to be out of the woods, I fell into a coma where I stayed for nearly a week. They couldn't figure it out. My vitals were regular, my brain scans showed normal function; and my fever was gone. My room had become a revolving door for hospital personnel, my friends and family, and even the general public, at least until my car was discovered.

After that I had a police officer posted outside my door 24/7, per Henderson's orders. It was while I was delirious that Sandy showed up. I remembered seeing Sandy, my monkey with the same eyes dangling from their sockets, at some point and even vaguely recalled a young thin man placing him on the table beside my bed and saying, 'It's over now.' but I couldn't be sure. Those couple days are a part of my life that I probably will never remember correctly because of the devastating fever that consumed me.

I wished the person who found me had left his name so I could thank him. On second thought, another epiphany crossed my mind. What if it was him, the serial killer? What if he called it in so he could indulge in the pleasure of killing me with his own hands? He last had Sandy. Maybe, it was he who had brought him back now, after all of these years? He was the only person who it could have been...

Eilida

Eilida no longer needed Sunshine, as she had simply been a vehicle her mind manufactured to deal with and sort through the tragedy she experienced. All the people and places she had been over the past nine days were a collection of reality mixed with figments of Eilida's imagination, caveats to direct her thoughts and lead her to the answers. The only exception was her mom who displayed herself in a ghost form to guide her to the past. She now remembered everything and Sunshine faded into a back corner of Eilida's mind in a safe pocket away from the specters and goblins, where hopefully she would forever stay.

Epilogue

The front page of the newspaper read *Man Found Dead in Motel… approximate age 35-40 was found dead late Friday evening. He was naked on the bed in a pool of his own blood. His throat had been slit. There were no signs of forced entry, his killer unknown.*

A few days later the newspaper read *Man Found Dead in Motel has been identified.* It further went on to read that the man, identified as 38 year old Evan O'Conner, was found dead in a motel room. He was a pharmaceutical salesman who traveled all over the country. He had no wife or children, and had no known living relatives. Preliminary results showed no fingerprints or DNA left at the scene from the killer. There was a picture beside the article. He was bald with dark and loathsome eyes. The evil in them stared from beyond the paper and beyond the grave.

Within a few more days the newspaper read Evan O'Conner Victim or Killer. Evan O'Conner had brutally killed his mother, father and brother at age 10. When police arrived on the scene he was raping his own mother as she lay dead, her throat slit. He was then sent to the state mental institution for evaluation. Evidence suggested his mother had been sexually molesting him. He had a younger sister who was found alive, hidden under her dresser.

The latest newspaper read *Evan O'Conner, Hurricane Killer?* A witness, a survivor from Hurricane Chloe, a category 4 Hurricane that struck Billows Hollow more than 20 years ago came forward and identified Evan O'Conner as the man who had slain her family. She had been the sole survivor and was found in a wooden chest inside what had been her parents' closet… His killer still unknown…

Detective Burkhalder sat on the floor of her house with her back against the couch, her legs spread out before her. She had the newspaper clippings sprawled out on the floor, and a glass of rum beside her.

She thought, *in my backyard, under my watch, he killed my good friend Jim Tate. We had known each other since first grade. All these years and early retirement, my mind couldn't rest until justice had been served. All Evan's dirty secrets will be exposed, all my research. Maybe now his victims' families can have closure. I can now sleep at night knowing he will never again take the lives of innocent people. But who took his life...* hung at the edge of her mind.

Volume 1 Ruthless Storm Trilogy

Eilida's Natal Chart and Reading via Patrice Renard (seen in Volume 2 Calm Before the Storm Evan's Sins).

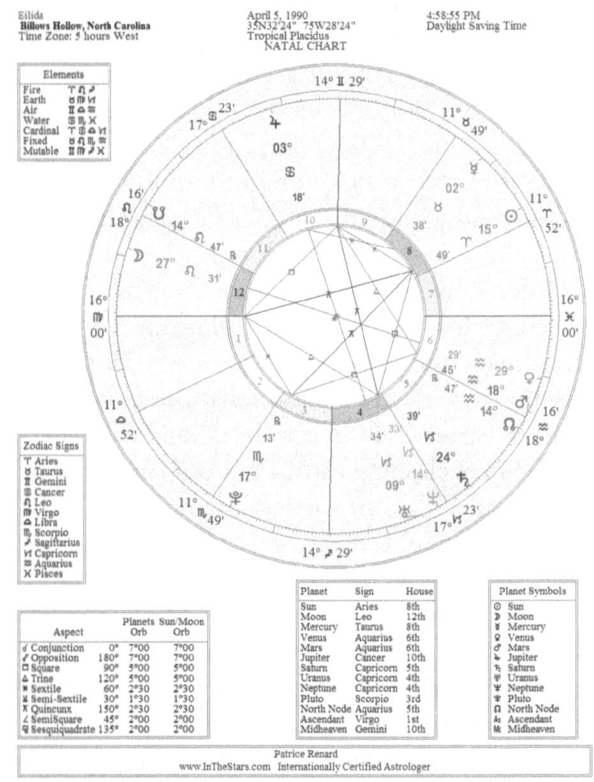

Volume 1 Ruthless Storm Trilogy

The Cosmo Natal Report for

Eilida
April 5, 1990
4:58:55 PM
Billows Hollow, North Carolina

Calculated for:
Daylight Savings Time,   Time Zone 5 hours West
Latitude: 35 N 32 24   Longitude: 75 W 28 24

Positions of Planets at Birth:

Sun	15 Ari 49	Pluto	17 Sco 13
Moon	27 Leo 31	N. Node	14 Aqu 47
Mercury	2 Tau 38	Asc.	16 Vir 00
Venus	29 Aqu 29	MC	14 Gem 29
Mars	18 Aqu 45	2nd cusp	11 Lib 52
Jupiter	3 Can 18	3rd cusp	11 Sco 49
Saturn	24 Cap 39	5th cusp	17 Cap 23
Uranus	9 Cap 34	6th cusp	18 Aqu 16
Neptune	14 Cap 33		

Chapter 1: How You Approach Life and How You Appear To Others

Virgo Rising:

Modest, unobtrusive, and often rather quiet or shy, you are a person who is content to be in the background or to serve as an assistant, in the supporting role rather than in the lead. You are quite humble in your own assessment of yourself and you have a very strong perfectionistic attitude, with a tendency to be overly self-critical. No matter how well you do something, you always see the flaws in it and how it could be improved. Often you will simply refuse to attempt something because you feel you cannot meet your own high standards.

You have an eye for detail and get upset when something is not done just so, usually something others consider rather inconsequential or trivial. You are hard to please and your relationships with others may suffer because of this. You also have refined sensitivities and are very discriminating and particular in your choice of foods, clothes, friends, artwork, etc. Order in your environment is very important to you.

You step into situations rather cautiously,

and not without realistically assessing all of the risks and potential advantages involved. Unless something is a safe bet, you are unlikely to dive into it. You tend to underestimate your own capacities and to lack confidence and trust in life, which inhibits your spontaneity. Worrying is a bad habit of yours. On the other hand, you rarely fall flat on your face and what you do, you do very well.

Others see you as a self-sufficient and rather self-contained person. You have a strong sense of propriety. Politeness, good manners, and correct behavior are important to you. Your clear, cool, objective and nonemotional attitude is apparent to others first, and though you are really quite helpful and caring, you do not radiate much sympathy so that others may not see the helpful side as readily. You may seem more businesslike and factual, and also more conservative, than you really are at heart. You are the person others might go to for technical advice or an unbiased opinion, but not for emotional support.

You are keenly observant, intelligent, and have a great desire for learning and for self-improvement, but you are not especially ambitious and are often satisfied in a rather simple, unglamorous position in life.

Chapter 2: The Inner You: Your Real Motivation

Sun in Aries:

You are a person who thrives on challenge, and you often feel that you must battle your way through life, depending upon no one and nothing but your own strength, intelligence, and courage. You believe in being totally honest, true to oneself and one's own vision and convictions, even if that means standing alone. Honesty, integrity, personal honor, and authenticity are your gods, and you have no sympathy for weakness of character in others.

You crave the freedom to do things in your own way, and you work very well independently. Cooperating with others or carrying out another's will is not your style. You like to be the chief - or to go it alone.

You love action and if others are settling down into a nice, comfortable little rut, then you are always ready to stir things up, do something new, make changes, bring in some fresh blood. Routine and sameness are like death to you. You are not afraid of trying something that's never been done before, and even though you may be seen as a fool sometimes, you also discover, invent, and initiate things that others will later emulate. Taking risks and following your own star are the breath of life for you, and you wilt (or get very frustrated and angry) if you cannot do this.

You are spontaneous, impulsive, direct, enthusiastic, and assertive. You believe in the power of positive thinking and positive action, and you think of yourself as a strong person - even invincible. You hate being ill or in any way in a position of dependency. Accepting your own human limitations and emotional needs is often difficult for you.

You are basically aggressive in your attitudes and have less facility in the receptive arts of relating to others, picking up subtle messages and nuances, listening, nurturing, and harmonizing. Often you are so fired up about your own projects or goals that you inadvertently run over or ignore other people's feelings and interests. Being receptive and appreciative of others' contributions, ideas, and feelings would go a long way in improving your relationships. Your impatience to get on with things causes you to be rather insensitive, and to therefore alienate others unnecessarily. You also frequently try to accomplish your ends by using anger or some version of a temper tantrum. You would gain much by learning to slow down, relax, and just let things be sometimes, but your energetic, restless nature rarely allows you to do this.

Sun in 8th house:

You crave intense experiences and are attracted to aspects of life that are strange, unfathomable, or taboo. You may hide your interests or inclinations, except from those who know you very intimately. You are rarely content with yourself and your life, and you have an inner urge to be continually going farther or deeper than you ever have before. You also have a strong interest in social power and the role that money and economics play in people's lives.

Sun Square Neptune:

You are extremely sensitive and imaginative, and you can get lost in your dreams, fantasies, and visions. You are attracted to artistic and creative pursuits, the world of color, beauty, and emotion. You are also drawn to mysticism and have deep spiritual aspirations and yearnings. Gentle and peace-loving, you may lack the will and competitive spirit needed to make your way in the world. You are often impractical and may seek to avoid or escape the hard realities of life.

Sun Sextile Mars:

You are positive, vital, energetic, active, a go-getter. You enjoy competition, and your initiative and self-confidence make you a winner.

Chapter 3: Mental Interests and Abilities

Mercury in Taurus:

Your mind operates in a very deliberate and methodical manner and you dislike being rushed or forced to give an opinion before you have thoroughly ruminated and digested an idea. You are also difficult to influence once your mind is made up.

Though slower to grasp new concepts or learn new skills, you are patient and persevering and, in fact, often become quite adept at whatever you put your mind and hand to, for you are willing to devote much time and attention to it. You succeed not so much because of your mental brilliance, but because you have the ability to concentrate and follow a project through to its completion. You have an aptitude for singing or drawing.

Mercury in 8th house:

The mysterious and the unknown fascinate you and you may investigate the supernatural or something that is hidden or taboo. You need to know what is going on behind the scenes. You are also deeply curious about or astute about economic, political, or social power, big business, and the motives and powers behind the social facade.

Mercury Sextile Venus:

You appreciate aesthetics and have a fine sense of form, design, and beauty. You could develop great technical skill as an artist, designer, craftsman, or creative writer. You could also sell objects of beauty - artistic products, cosmetics, jewelry, etc.

You have the ability to please and harmonize well with others and have a talent for assuaging strain in the relationship of two other people. Your sense of humor, tact, and personal charm are a great benefit to you in any work with people on a one-to-one level.

Mercury Sextile Jupiter:

You have an ongoing interest in learning and expanding your mental horizons. You enjoy traveling, philosophical discussions, and exchanging ideas with those of different experiences and viewpoints. Broad-minded and fair, you are well-suited to law, consulting, diplomatic relations, and also business. You learn quickly, and can pick up on a new idea or concept with relative ease.

Chapter 4: Emotions: Moods, Feelings, Romance

Moon in Leo:

Warm, loving, and generous in your affections, you inspire tremendous devotion and loyalty in your loved ones. This is good, since you would never settle for anything less! You want to be adored and worshipped like the king or queen that you feel you are, and it is difficult for anyone to resist the warmth and attention you lavish on those you care about. You have a great deal of pride and need to be recognized and appreciated. The way to really hurt your feelings is to ignore you. You are genuine, sincere, and have a strong sense of personal integrity. You hate emotional games and dishonesty.

Moon in 12th house:

Your own feelings and emotions are something of an enigma to you, and it is often difficult for you to share with others what you are feeling.

You frequently withdraw from contact with the world, and need a healing, peaceful environment in order to blossom and come out of yourself.

You identify with the oppressed, disenfranchised or underdog in any situation and want to help them or care for them in some way.

Moon Opposition Venus:

You have conflicting emotional desires and needs which complicate your personal life. You may feel that you cannot depend on your love partner to take care of you or perhaps you cannot decide what you really want in a love relationship: a parent or a lover. If your needs for emotional sustenance and love are not satisfied, overeating (especially sweets) can be a problem for you.

Venus in Aquarius:

You are open and unconventional in your attitude towards love, romance, and sex. You enjoy socializing, bringing people together, and having many friends of both sexes. You value friendship very highly and are, in fact, more comfortable being a friend than a lover. You desire an intellectual rapport or spiritual bond with your love partner, but deep intimacy and emotional bonding do not come easily to you. The role of "husband" or "wife" in the traditional sense doesn't appeal to you, and you abhor jealousy and possessiveness since you feel that no person truly "belongs" to another. You appreciate a love partner who will allow you plenty of freedom and is not very emotionally demanding.

Venus in 6th house:

When you care about someone, you like to serve them, doing small thoughtful favors, helping them, or doing something tangible to show your affection.

You also have considerable artistic or creative skill and may sew or do other handiwork or crafts. In fact, you are suited for a profession involving beauty or pleasure or making people happy in some way.

Venus Trine Jupiter:

You appreciate beautiful surroundings and congenial company, and though you enjoy helping people, you will rarely put yourself out too much in order to do so. You are good-humored and generous at heart but inclined to be lazy.

Chapter 5: Drive and Ambition: How You Achieve Your Goals

Mars in Aquarius:

You are very socially oriented and work well in cooperation with others. You may be active in community affairs or unite with others of similar ideals and intentions to work toward a common goal. Progressive and democratic, you are not concerned with hoarding personal power or having authority over others. You are a team player.

New, unconventional methods appeal to you, especially ideas that involve bringing people together or creating fairer working conditions - such as networking, profit-sharing, job-sharing, etc. New technologies also interest you.

Your energy level is high but somewhat erratic. You can be impatient, rebellious, and inconstant in pursuing your aims.

Mars in 6th house:

You expect to work hard for anything you accomplish and you have no patience for people who don't pull their own weight. Work is a passion for you at times, and you push yourself too hard. You can be too demanding of the people you work with also.

If your energy is not invested in a job or career, you can become a fanatic about your health, and you may exercise or "work out" vigorously and perhaps excessively.

Mars Square Pluto:

You have a powerful will and when you want something, you pursue it passionately and relentlessly until you achieve it. You may be so driven by your desire that you lose all objectivity. You often become compulsive, even obsessed, with doing or achieving something, no matter what the costs or how hard you must work for it. Your forcefulness may be veiled or subtle, for often you do not reveal your real aims and intentions to others until they cross you. Intense power struggles and relationships with a strong dominance/submissiveness theme are likely. You have enormous energy reserves, and are capable of extraordinary effort and great achievement if you use your energies for constructive purposes.

Chapter 6: Other Influences

Jupiter in Cancer:

You make others feel accepted and comfortable. You have a knack for breaking down feelings of alienation and you make others feel included and a part of group activities. You have a loving, protective side that wants to take care of everyone. Creating a supportive atmosphere that is nourishing both to yourself and to others is one of your strengths.

Also, your home and heritage are important to you, and you maintain close connections to your past.

Jupiter in 10th house:

Your career or contribution to the world at large is likely to touch many people's lives in a very positive, helpful way. You aim high and have an innate confidence and trust both in your own abilities and in life in general, which enables you to go far. You want to do something BIG with your life, and you attract the support you need to do so, for your aims are not solely for your own personal benefit. You want to give something back to the world, or to improve others' lives as well as your own.

Saturn in Capricorn:

You have a great capacity for self-denial in the pursuit of a long-range goal. You are capable of hard work and persistent labor, but you may lack joyfulness and the ability to play. You often feel burdened by life's demands and responsibilities, and may envy those who seem to attract what they want in life without a great deal of personal effort.

There is a very judgmental, stern, and uncompromising side of yourself which may inhibit you a great deal. You must avoid becoming heavy and cynical, or becoming a rather callous, sophisticated adult whose practicality and realism squeeze out the playful, imaginative side of life.

Saturn in 5th house:

It may be difficult for you to play spontaneously or just let your hair down, for you tend to inhibit that side of yourself by being too self-conscious and concerned with the impression you are making.

You may work very hard at some sport or creative medium in order to excel, for you want very, very much to be noticed, acknowledged, and recognized as special in some way. Though you may indeed be outstanding, you also need to learn to relax and enjoy yourself more.

Uranus in Capricorn:

You are part of a 7 year group of people who are active in reforming businesses, governments, and other large social structures. A great deal of streamlining and reorganizing takes place, most of which will help to improve the well-being of people, the ultimate goal of these reforms. Your generation will promote various reforms that will vary in different nations. For example, some will increase socialization of public services and others will put more services in the hands of private industry. In either case, your generation strives for greater efficiency and a great deal of waste is eliminated from industry and government.

Uranus in 4th house:

Your childhood or your relationship with your parents was unsettling or unstable in some way, so that you may never have felt that you had firm ground beneath your feet. One of your parents may have been unusual, eccentric, or an inconstant influence in your life. Abrupt changes in location or in family relationships may have made you feel insecure, but positively you were given more freedom and less pressure to conform to conventions, which enables you to be more of an individual and less tethered to restrictive ideas of how one "should" behave, feel, or live.

Uranus Conjunct Neptune:

You were also born during a period that lasted approximately 5 years and is characterized by an unusually high degree of imagination and sensitivity. You are part of a group of people who are very inspired but also unstable. Many unusual contributions to the arts, music, religion, and psychic development are brought forth from your age group. These works are often strange and bizarre, and always original. Your age group also inspires intense political movements that are often fanatical or unreasonable in their goals.

Neptune in Capricorn:

You are part of a 14 year group of people who are conservative and traditional in spiritual aspirations and religious outlook. Your age group returns to some traditional basics in religion, and also traditional styles in music and art. Classical music and literature have a revival with your age group, and a great deal of inspiration is gained from the masters of arts, music, literature, and philosophy throughout history. Your age group is contemplative and reflective about religious matters and you take an objective and logical approach to religious issues. Many of you are cynics and critics of spiritual and metaphysical ideas.

Other age groups criticize your group for not having enough heart and compassion. Sometimes this is true and is evidenced by some unusually crafty and manipulative fraud and deception that occurs in the higher ranks of governments and large businesses.

Neptune in 4th house:

Your childhood and early home life were colored by a great deal of confusion or by people with unusually active imaginations, aspirations, or fantasies. It is difficult for you to see your childhood and your relationship with your parents in a clear, realistic light. You may search for the ideal, loving home you wish you had, or believe you had, when you were a child. Finding inner peace and a sense of emotional security within yourself is important to you.

Volume 1 Ruthless Storm Trilogy

Neptune Sextile Pluto:

The entire generation to which you belong has tremendous opportunities for spiritual rebirth and awakening. This will not be forced upon you or precipitated by unavoidable events, rather it comes from an inner yearning and a natural propensity to seek the depths.

Pluto in Scorpio:

You are part of a 12 year group of people who have a complex and deep emotional side. Your age group has a great fascination for the mysteries of life, and members of your age group will make extraordinary breakthroughs in the understanding of life processes; major advances in biological sciences will open up new technological possibilities. Intensive probing into genetic structure and cellular processes will accelerate genetic engineering into new vistas. Your generation also probes the mysteries of birth and death, and members of your age group will even develop laboratories for forging new understanding of what happens at birth and death. Other breakthroughs will be made in the understanding of animal behavior and sexual activity. Archeological studies will unearth vast new insights into the history of man, and the exploration of the ocean will receive a new impetus, spurred by unusual and interesting findings made at the bottom of the sea.

Behind all of this work is the deep, probing, penetrating interest in the mysterious. There is a deep fascination with sex, power, and the occult as well. Hypnosis, karate, and other mental and physical training techniques are likely to be very popular with your age group. The love of mystery is also likely to bring a revival of mystery novels and movies; your age group will bring the macabre into current fashion and style.

You are an emotionally complex group, and you can be prone to some very strange behavior. Intrigue and mystery are exciting to your age group, and hopefully this does not get the better of you, causing you to act in a cruel or grotesque manner. There is a chance that crime, violence, and emotional disturbance will be relatively high in your age group, but hopefully your interest in the mysterious, strange, grotesque, and macabre will not manifest in this way.

Pluto in 3rd house:

You have a probing, penetrating mind and are highly analytical and critical in your thinking. Work that involves research, investigating mysteries or hidden causes, or deep study and analysis suits you very well.

You are also a convincing speaker, bringing others around to your own point of view by the intensity of your convictions.

Sun, Pluto, Ascendant Yod

Something that occurred in your past, most likely during your childhood, had an intense and life-changing effect on you. Resolving this old issue will ultimately have a strong, transformational influence at a deep, personal level.

Teaser

The police escorted Evan to Windy Oaks Mental Facility for evaluation where he spent the next eight years of his life as a ward. He was a model patient, always followed the rules, and never stepped out of line, not once did he give them any reason to believe their treatments weren't working or that his soul had been so devastated it couldn't be 'cured'.

On the outside his demeanor was calm and even amiable but inside the winds raged and howled. He learned control as a child, but it was clouded by an all-consuming fear and hate. Now he soaked up the skills and learned what he so desperately coveted and would make him one of the most elusive, sought after, vicious, and calculating serial killers of all time.

His desire to finish the job he started weighted heavy on his battle ridden heart. His mother's presence grew and consumed him. He beat himself up over his lack of control, his impulse youthful behavior that cost him closure - the peace and serendipity he yearned for. He observed and plotted the path of his life. A detailed plan with no room for lack of control or foolish, childish behavior.

The blackness of his heart evident in his eyes - endless pits of darkness.

At eighteen Windy Oaks released into society with a monthly check, a prescription, a college schedule, a group home, and two years of outpatient treatment to assist him in daily living and coping skills.

Alice Burkhalder hunts him. All the evidence she has is circumstancial, none-the-less she beilives he is the Hurricane Killer. Does she get to Evan first or is it someone else? Someone who has a larger vendetta against him.

Keep reading for an excerpt of the cat and mouse thriller!

Excerpt from The Calm Before the Storm

You're Headin' the Wrong Way

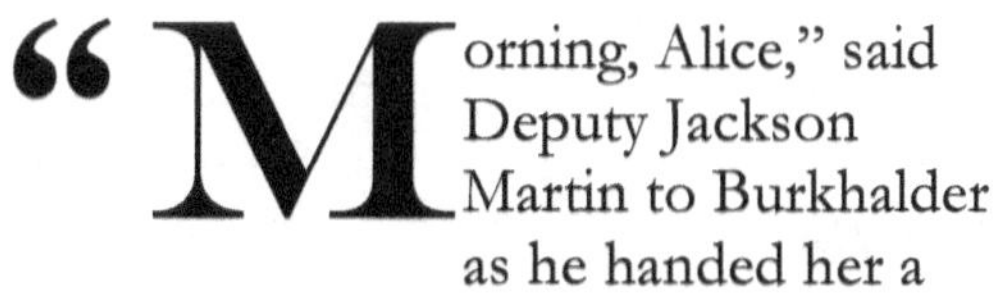

"**M**orning, Alice," said Deputy Jackson Martin to Burkhalder as he handed her a much needed cup of coffee.

"Black the way ya like."

Burkhalder's mind reminisced on the mornings she awoke in his bed, fresh coffee brewing in the kitchen. "You're a life saver Jax." He didn't allow anyone but her to call him Jax. It was her nickname for him since they met in the third grade.

He loved how the morning light bounced off the red highlights in her auburn hair. "You reckon Tate's stayin' on the island?"

"Jim wouldn't have it any other way. He built a special reinforced closet he keeps stocked with supplies. Thinkin' we should pay him a visit later." Burkhalder, Jim, and Jax grew up together. It was only in the past few months Jax and Alice had started seeing each other.

Through the bumper to bumper cars sunlight glinted off a young man's head from across the street from where Alice and Jax were having their discussion, catching Jax's eye. "What's that kid doin'? We need people off this island not walkin' towards it."

"You stay, I'll take care of it. See you later. What do say to a romantic night at a hurricane shelter?" Joked Burkhalder.

"You got it babe, after we visit Jim."

Burkhalder winked and headed across the street, placing her hand out for cars to let her through.

Evan noted the carrot top cop heading his direction. He ignored her, keeping a steady pace. Neither she nor anyone else would stop his mission.

"Young man!" Evan heard her call. He wanted to continue ignoring her but knew it best to treat her with respect - avoid confrontation. *Control.* Evan halted his pace. "Yes, ma'am." *She's no more than a few years older than me. Where does she get off calling me young man?*

"Help me out. We need you heading off the island not towards it. There's a hurricane headin' our way."

He looked at the peaceful sky above him. "Certainly doesn't appear that way."

A creeping blackness took over his pale blue eyes, causing Burkhalder to look away and avoid being sucked into the dark abyss. She looked back and his normal color returned. *Get hold of yourself. It's your imagination.* "The calm before the storm. Never looks like a hurricane until it hits. These islands get mighty dangerous so I suggest you head back towards the mainland or to the shelter." She scribbled the address in her cop issue notepad and handed it to him. "Take a right at the light then walk three blocks. Shelter's on the left."

He hated their accents and considered Billows Hollow residents as nothing more than undereducated redneck hicks.

Evan resisted the urge to knock her in the head. Instead, he smiled. "Thank you. I guess I'll be headin' that way." He felt her eyes on his back so he followed her directions and made the right, continued on for a block soaking in the dense vegetation then veered through the home-lined streets. Nothing would stop his mission.

Something about the young man, more than his black-pit eyes, didn't sit well with Burkhalder although she couldn't put her finger on it. She made a note to check with the shelter later.

The Tates

Jim Tate piled up the outdoor furniture and carried it to the shed. His deep brown tangles matted and drenched from sweat. His raven-haired wife's liquid blue eyes watched her husband's tanned muscular build work in the morning sun. The sun she knew would soon be replaced by swirling clouds and gale force winds.

"Mommy, can I go outside and help daddy?"

"Evie, how about you help mommy?"

"I'm not a little boy. If Ely can help how come I can't?" He stomped his feet. "I want to help daddy." Lilly looked into her son's eyes. At seven years of age he thought he was a man.

She kneeled and leveled her eyes with his, handing him a stack of plates. "Setting the table will help daddy. He's going to be hungry when he comes inside."

"O... K..." Hesitant, Evie set the plates on the table and silverware beside each plate. When he finished he scrambled to the refrigerator, opened the door, grabbed two bottles of chilly water, and ran towards the front door. "Bringing daddy and Ely water!"

Lilly shook her head, closed the refrigerator door, then watched her youngest son, brown curls flying and bouncy as he ran, hand his father and brother a bottle of water. She read Jim's lips deciphering his words. "Thank you, Evie!" He patted his head and handed him a bucket of beach toys. Jim in the lead, the boys in tow, strutted towards the shed, arms loaded with the last of their outdoor furniture.

Lilly smiled and admired her two year old daughter, Eilida. Her brown curls tied up in a *Pebbles* bow. "Don't grow up too quick, sweetie. Mommy's little girl." Eilida smiled, melting Lilly's heart.

Eilida dropped the last of her toys on the floor. "Oopsie!"

"Oopsie!" Mimicked Lilly, laughing at her daughter's uh-oh expression and widened eyes. She unlatched the highchair and picked up her daughter. "Let's see what daddy and the boys are doing."

"OK, Mommy."

Evan

Telltale hair grass and beach grass jutted upwards from the sandy coastline. Thanks to the meddling Carrot Top Cop he made it to the island quicker than if he'd stayed on the main road. Most of the homes were vacant, so he traipsed through open yards. The sunny sky still gave no sign of Hurricane Chloe's approach. He took his shoes off, rolled the bottoms of his pants up and stepped onto the sandy coast. The calm, peaceful water told the same lie as the sky.

Every house looked the same to him. They all belonged to over-privileged assholes who evacuated at the first hint of a "hurricane". The perfect circumstances for him, he didn't need people around, just one family. The island looked like a ghost town. Huge homes loomed to his left and the coastline to his right.

He followed the curvy coastline looking for signs of life. The sound of hammering caught his attention. At first he wasn't sure if it was phantom sounds his mind conjured or real. The closer he got to the sound he realized it was real. Mingled between hammering he heard voices, one of them sounded like Carrot Top Cop. He stood still, craned his neck and listened. Two men and a woman. Evan strolled towards the voices and stood stock still as Carrot Top's windblown hair shadowed his view of the men.

"Anybody thirsty?" The sound emanated from nowhere. A woman with raven black hair tied into a pony tail walked into Evan's view. To stay hidden, he climbed the steps of a vacant two-story home and sat on the wooden porch he imagined would be all but gone by night's end. The slats of the porch afforded him a view of the group and the wind carried their voices in his direction. Both cops from earlier and a young couple.

"Thanks, honey." Lilly gave her husband a kiss as he grabbed a glass filled with lemonade off the tray.

"Reckon that was the last one," said Jax, lowering the hammer in his hand.

"Jackson, Alice, come inside, sit a spell."

"Jim, we ain't got time. Just wantin' to make sure you, Lilly, and the kids were ready. See if you needed 'nythin'. Try and change your mind. Plenty of room at the shelter."

Burkhalder snapped her fingers and looked towards Jax. "You reminded me. I need to check on that kid we saw earlier. It'll have ta wait, we need to secure the area." The breeze picked up and clouds swam past them. "Be startin' soon," said Burkhalder, peering towards the sky, shading her eyes with her hand.

Two little brown-haired boys chased each other across the sandy beach tossing a football. It landed near the tall, blond cop they called Jackson. He picked up the ball, ran a few yards then hocked it into the air. Both boys ran after it. *Like dogs playing fetch. Two boys - lucky day.*

Evan's mother's face appeared on the dark-haired woman as she mouthed to Evan *I love you.* She reached her hand towards him. *I hate you, you rancid bitch!* The dark-haired woman turned back to herself and his mother disappeared. Not sure if he yelled aloud or to himself, he peered through the slats. The group hugged and said their goodbyes. If he shouted out loud nobody noticed.

Evan rested his hands on the wooden flanks in front of him. A loose board bobbled beneath his palm. He pried it upward and reached beneath - a key. Amazed at his unbelievable dumb luck he tried the key in the door. *What dumb-asses.* He marched right into their house and rummaged through their mail piled on a sleek black table beside the door. Every letter addressed to Robert and/or Margaret Plum - he noted their names. He took in the house decorated in a modern theme of high-end black and white furniture. Recessed ceiling lights flicked on and off automatically as he walked into and out of each room. A large, custom designed shower in the upstairs master bedroom caught his attention. A slew of ideas coursed through his head.

He cracked the front door and peered outside. The cops had left. Now was his chance. He closed the door and went out the back, the way he came in, and strolled by the dark-haired family's house. The father and brothers continued to toss the football. It rolled beside Evan's feet. He picked it up and handed it to the littlest boy.

With big blue eyes, the boy looked up at him. "Thanks!" Then he ran to his brother's side.

The father walked towards Evan and extended his hand. "Name's Jim, didn't know anyone else stayed on the island."

Evan, remembering the manners and appropriate behavior he learned at Windy Oaks, shook Jim's hand. Using his real name was out of the question and so was the name Kevin. *The blasted girl may show up again.* "Nyle, nice to meet ya." He hated the southern redneck talk but knew they'd be more welcoming if he used it. He'd almost considered using the name *Bubba* but figured the man might take that as mocking.

"Nyle, you stayin' on the island?"

"Lookin' after my uncle's house. He's payin' me good to keep it up."

"Who's your uncle?"

Nosy bastard aren't you? Evan expected that question and hoped Jim and the Plums weren't real good friends. "Robert Plum."

"The Plums. They just bought that place. Had some remodelin' done."

"It's right nice inside. More luxury than I got at home." Evan drew up his face on one side as he mouthed the words. "What do you mak-a this storm?" The sun beat hot and steady on the men as they talked.

"We go through this every couple-few years. Storm's s'posed to head south. Got a reinforced room, if it gets bad enough you're welcome to join us."

Evan felt the sweat beading on his forehead and bubbling on his chest and legs. "Appreciate the offer. I'll keep it in mind, Jim." The football rolled to Evan's feet.

If psychological torment and horror is your cup of tea try out the Evan's Girls series. Each story the life of a young lady who lost her family to the gruesome murders from one serial killer.

Keep reading for the first chapter of Scarlett Volume 1 Evan's Girls.

Scarlett

Chapter 1
Pseudo

April 1961 5 years old

The sunny day in April carried a light breeze as I jumped off the last step on the bus. No sign that the hot summer was approaching quickly. My blue apron skirt bounced with the spring in my step and my saddle shoes beat against the pavement as I ran towards my mommy waiting at the front door.

She leaned down, her skirt brushing the cement walkway and wrapped her arms around me. "Hi, baby."

"Hi, Mommy. Look what I made today," I said with pride as I lifted a large purple paper butterfly from my backpack.

"Oh, isn't that beautiful," she said with surprise in her voice. "Let's hang that in your room, shall we?"

"Yes, yes," I agreed and rushed toward my room. The white walls garnered many butterflies of every color and size. My twin bed had a lavender comforter covered with purple and white butterflies and lavender curtains hung across the windows. My room was a haven made of my favorite color – purple. I stood by the spot where I wanted Mommy to hang my new butterfly.

She entered the room, her yellow skirt flounced at her knees with each step she took. Her dark hair tied up in a ponytail and her bright brown eyes smiled at me. "This is where you want it?"

"Uh huh."

She took a thumbtack and pinned the butterfly to the spot I pointed at. "There you are. We'll show Daddy when he gets home." Her smile large and full of love.

"OK," I said, bouncing into the kitchen for my after school snack.

The sun lowered in the sky and Daddy came home. As soon as I heard the door open I rushed toward him and he scooped me into his thick arms filled with tickling hair. "How was your day?" he asked, his hazel eyes beamed with joy and sparkled in the setting light of the sun. His blond hair slicked back against his oval head.

"Good. I want to show you what I made."

"I must see it," he said in mock surprise.

"Mommy hung it in my room."

He hoisted me over his head and sat me square on his shoulders as we headed down the hallway. He entered the room.

"Do you see it, Daddy?" I asked.

"No," he said spinning around and making me dizzy. "Is it here?" he asked, stopping and pointing to an old butterfly.

I giggled. This was our routine. "No, Daddy."

He spun again, then asked again before he settled on the new one.

"It's just gorgeous, almost as pretty as you – my little butterfly." He lowered me.

I smiled a partially toothless smile. "I love you, Daddy."

"I love you. Hmm… where is my other love?" he said, asking about Mommy.

"I think she's finishing dinner."

He widened his eyes. "Oh, let's sneak up on her," he said, tiptoeing down the hallway and placing a finger over his mouth.

I stifled a chuckle and followed on my tiptoes. We peeked around the corner and Mommy gazed our way. "Oh, what do we have here?" she said, her eyes wide as if in surprise.

I giggled and Daddy wrapped his arms around her, planting a kiss on her lips.

It was a Friday and Genevieve, our elderly neighbor, came over about seven p.m. as always so my parents could enjoy date night. I couldn't pronounce her name so I called her Gen. She wore her white hair in a bun and had kind blue eyes.

When the bell rang I rushed toward it and flung the door wide open. "Don't you look pretty," she said.

"Thank you," I answered, spinning in my purple nightgown.

"Genevieve, come in," voiced my daddy.

She stepped inside and took a seat with me at the kitchen table. I had the cards already out and waiting. I so enjoyed Friday nights and our card games, which she usually let me win.

My parents kissed my head and walked out the door.

Gen's blue eyes gazed into mine. "One day you will do something great. Very few people have eyes like yours and they give you a special oomph that others don't have."

I smiled. Gen loved my eyes. One was green and the other amber. She and my parents agreed that I was something superior like a fairy. They insisted my eyes gave me special powers.

After an hour of cards Gen tucked me into bed. "Goodnight, Scarlett," she whispered, planting a gentle kiss on my cheek.

I woke up hours later to a large commotion in the house and the sound of Gen crying. Scared and worried, thinking Gen was hurt, I jumped out of bed and scurried down the hallway, halting at the end of it. A police officer dressed in uniform sat beside Gen on the couch. She was OK but where were my parents?

My heart thumped against my ribcage. Another officer walked into the house, his eyes rested on me.

"How are you?" asked the officer. His mustache moved up and down with the motions of his mouth. He steadily walked towards me as I backed down the hallway. Flashes of fear and unidentifiable blood-smeared images rattled my mind.

"I need you to come with me," he said, getting closer with his hand out. I gazed into his dark eyes. There was no sparkle inside them. My heart beat faster when he took another step. Remembering the games I played with Daddy, I side-stepped him. His hand grabbed for mine when I slid underneath his legs, ran as fast as my two small feet carried me and jumped onto Gen's lap. Wrapping my arms around her neck, I clung for my life.

I don't know what scared me so much, but an ominous sensation entered my gut and I knew my life was about to change for the worse. I should have woken up to Mommy and Daddy giggling not Gen's sobs and two unknown people in my house. They wore badges but to me they were strangers.

"Shhh... Scarlett," Gen soothed as I scrambled to plaster myself against her.

"She has to come with us," said the officer in a deep voice.

"She's a little girl and confused. I will go with her," Gen said, her arms wrapped around my trembling body.

"Suit yourself," the deep-voiced officer huffed.

"Where's Mommy and Daddy," I whispered in Gen's ear.

"Oh, Scarlett. You sweet baby. Your mommy and daddy..." she choked back a sob, "they aren't coming home."

I traced the flowered pattern on the couch with my finger as her words sunk in. "Why not?" I asked, my brows furrowed.

"They've gone to heaven," Gen responded in a gentle voice as she caressed the back of my head.

I didn't really understand. "Without me?"

Gen took a deep breath. "Yes but it wasn't their choice. Their time on Earth has passed but you still have a job to do." She lifted the hair above my ear and whispered,

"Remember, one day you will do something magnificent."

I leaned back, still planted on her lap and looked into her blue eyes. "Because my eyes give me special powers."

"Yes," she chuckled, "because of your eyes."

Hand in hand with Gen I walked out of my home, never to return, and climbed into the back of the police car.

There were many things that happened within those few moments that I wouldn't understand until a few years later.